CLAWDEEN WOLF

X New Custom iridescent wrap dress
X A pack of brothers but no date for her Sassy Sixteen
X Purple halter dress, gold L.A.M.B. ankle boots

...is overshadowed by her six brothers and her fab friends, ...en plans to finally strut her stuff in the spotlight at her upcoming ...Sixteen bash. But then the Ghoul Next Door video goes viral, and it ... the woods for the family Wolf. Clawdeen goes stir-crazy hiding out ... her family's B&B with her annoying brothers until Lala shows up to keep her company. But is the vamp flirting with Claude?

FRANKIE STEIN

Frankie can't believe that Brett betrayed her. Just when she thought she had sparked a new romance, it seems to have fizzled out. Still, Frankie is charged up and ready to fight for her rights. She refuses to run for the hills, and since her face isn't shown in the video, she can afford to stay in Salem. Who's with her? . . . Hello? Anyone still here?

ME ODY CARVER

Me... wants to help put the smackdown on Bekka's Monster H... Tours, but she's kinda busy trying to get the truth out of her ...rents and keep Ms. J from sending Jackson into hiding. As sh... uggles to walk the line between normie and RAD, she starts to ...ize that people are actually listening to what she says – even C... e! Is Melody's newfound voice here to stay?

Fitting in is out.

Also by
LISI HARRISON

Monster High

Monster High
The Ghoul Next Door

The Clique

The Clique
Best Friends for Never
Revenge of the Wannabes
Invasion of the Boy Snatchers
The Pretty Committee Strikes Back
Dial L for Loser
It's Not Easy Being Mean
Sealed with a Diss

WHERE THERE'S A WOLF, THERE'S A WAY

A novel by

Lisi Harrison

www.atombooks.net

ATOM

First published in the United States in 2011 by Poppy,
an imprint of Little, Brown and Company
First published in Great Britain in 2011 by Atom

A CIP catalogue record for this book
is available from the British Library.

ISBN 978-1-907410-65-9

Printed and bound in Great Britain by
Clays Ltd, St Ives plc

Papers used by Atom are from well-managed forests
and other responsible sources.

MIX
Paper from
responsible sources
FSC
www.fsc.org   FSC® C104740

Atom
An imprint of
Little, Brown Book Group
100 Victoria Embankment
London EC4Y 0DY

An Hachette UK Company
www.hachette.co.uk

www.atombooks.net

Fur Cindy Lederman, Garrett Sander, Eric Hardie, and the rest of the freakishly creative Monster High team. You put the *awe* in *claw*.*

* If *claw* was spelled with an *e* on the end, this would have been so clever. Instead, it lands in the "A for effort" category. Which, by the way, starts with an *e*. Just saying.

TABLE OF CONTENTS

CHAPTER ONE
ON THE L.A.M.B.

The moon—a delicately arched crescent—was weeks away from being full. It was not time to hide. She was not transforming. Her monthly battle with rapid hair growth, insatiable hunger, and extreme irritability was not the issue. Still, Clawdeen Wolf was in a dark ravine, running for her life.

"Slow down!" she barked at the five athletic J.Crew catalog–worthy guys who formed a protective rhombus around her as they charged, panting, through the woods. Their mud-stained construction boots pounded the twig-covered earth with tireless determination. Not a minute passed without one of them vowing to keep Clawdeen safe, pledging to sacrifice his life for hers. It would have been extremely sweet—romantic, even—if they were contestants on *The Bachelorette*. But since they were her brothers, it was getting super annoying.

"My feet are killing me!" she groaned between breaths.

Howldon, aka Don, the oldest triplet by sixty-eight seconds, peered over his shoulder and looked down, fixing his orange-brown eyes on Clawdeen's pointy-toed gold ankle boots. "I'd kill you too if you stuffed me into those things." He turned to face the thicket ahead. "It's like the shoemaker only made room for one toe."

Howie, the middle triplet, snickered. If Howleen, or Leena, the youngest triplet, had been there, she would have seen Don's insult and doubled it. Leena—whose nickname rhymed with *mean-a* for a reason—had boot issues of her own, thanks to Arrowhead Boot Camp. While Clawdeen suffered from blisters, Leena's pain came from a drill sergeant, five AM whistles, and group meetings about anger management. *Ahhhh*...just thinking about her certifiable sister's yearlong sentence brought relief.

"They didn't come from a *shoemaker*!" Clawdeen practically spit. "They were designed by L.A.M.B."

"Is that why you're running so baaaaaaaad?" joked Clawnor from the back. His nickname was Nino because he tended to be "windy," like El Niño.

The Wolf brothers laughed.

"What's *your* excuse?" Clawdeen wanted to ask. But she already knew. Her sensitive canine ears heard the curses Nino muttered every time he ran into a branch.

Now thirteen, her youngest brother's fur was coming in fast. Nino's bushy brows, sideburns, and tangles of black hair undulated in front of his dark eyes like sea grass. It was nothing a bobby pin or styling products couldn't fix, but Nino refused. He had waited all his life for big-boy fur and wasn't about to let a few thwacks in the face bully him back to baldness.

"Owie," Clawdeen whimpered. The sting of a heel rubbed raw slowed her sprint to a gallop. *Is it hard to get blood out of leather? If only Lala were here. She'd know.* But none of her friends were around. That was the problem… well, one of them.

"Keep moving, Clawdeen," Rocks insisted, grabbing her wrist to pull her along. Leaves and long shadows blurred into bands of darkness. "We're almost there."

"This is so stupid." She limp-ran, holding up her purple halter dress. "We don't even know if anyone is chasing us and—"

"No, what's *stupid* is a girl running in lamb's boots," he snapped. "They were obviously made for hooves, not toes."

The boys howled with laughter. Clawdeen might have chuckled too if her feet weren't throbbing like techno. Instead, Rocks's insane remark became an excuse to stop running and glare at him.

Born Howlmilton, Clawdeen's younger brother got his nickname because of his dumb-as-rocks comments. But what he lacked in smarts, he made up for in speed—record-breaking, jowl-dropping, thirty-five-miles-per-hour speed. All he had to do to stay on the school track team—and retain his star status— was get straight Ds. Which he did, making the family's fastest member also the slowest.

"Keep moving!" Howie barked as the others forged ahead.

They took a lot of crap from the other RADs for their birth

names. But deep down, they had similar objections. Because, seriously, what had their parents been thinking? It's not like all normie kids were named Norman, Norma, Normandy, or Normiena. So why the need to force *Howl* and *Claw* on the Wolf kids? Being a girl with a hairy neck was embarrassing enough. Couldn't her parents have at least *tried* to make life less mortifying?

Rocks smacked Clawdeen's butt playfully. "Giddyup, *lamb*."

Growling, she started limping forward again, silently cursing the day for not turning out the way it was supposed to.

Thursday, October fourteenth, I curse you! You tricked me! From now on, my year has three hundred sixty-four days.

It wasn't supposed to happen like this. The itinerary had been solid. After school and a rigorous body wax, she, Lala, and Blue would take a limo to the Oregon sand dunes. There, they would meet up with Cleo and the accessories editor for *Teen Vogue*. First, a team of hair and makeup artists would glam Clawdeen, Blue, and Cleo into models. Under Lala's direction, stylists would adorn them in priceless jewels exhumed from Cleo's aunt's tomb. Next, the famed photographer Kolin VanVerbeentengarden would photograph them on camels for a fashion editorial layout on Cairo couture. After a toast to their futures in fashion, they would sneak tiny sips of champagne—aka "model water"—then limo back to Salem. The next day would be spent delighting their classmates with enviable anecdotes from the set. Months later, their exotic beauty would be available on newsstands everywhere—printed on high-gloss paper and bound by Condé Nast.

But the trio had never even made it to the sand dunes. They

never got glammed. They never sipped model water. And they would never be printed on high gloss.

Rue you, October fourteenth!

During the ride down, she, Lala, and Blue were searching the limo's flat screen for TMZ when they happened upon a special called "The Ghoul Next Door." It featured all three of them, plus Clawdeen's brother Clawd and many of their RAD friends. The never-before-seen glimpse into the secret lives of Salem's monsters was supposed to air only if their faces were blurred, homes obscured, and names omitted.

But there it was, clear as Crystal Light. In high def, no less. Not a single blur. Not a single black box. Their true identities—identities the RADs had struggled to keep hidden for generations—were broadcast all over town. Now, instead of celebrating at a wrap party, she was under wraps, limp-running all the way to the Wolf family's hideout.

Thursday the fourteenth is the new Friday the thirteenth!

Their faces were sure to be on the Internet and the AP wire by now. And the worst part? Cleo de Nile, Clawdeen's *ex*–best friend, must have had something to do with it. Because if proof really was in the pudding, this was one lumpy dessert.

Lump 1: Frankie Stein had played a big role in producing "The Ghoul Next Door," earning her major popularity points with the RADs. Cleo's queen bee status was threatened, so she was determined to take Frankie down.

Lump 2: Cleo had turned her back on the RADs and become overnight besties with Bekka Madden, a normie who was out to destroy Frankie Stein for stealing her man.

Lump 3: Cleo had refused to be in "The Ghoul Next Door," proving she knew it would expose the RADs.

It was hard to imagine Cleo jeopardizing the entire RAD community. But as Clawdeen's mother always said, "People do unimaginable things when they're insecure. Look at Heidi Pratts." Clawdeen got squirmy when her trying-to-be-hip mother referenced pop culture—especially when she got celebrities' names wrong. But Harriet was right: Cleo's insecurities, like Heidi's, had driven her toward the unimaginable.

Still, how could she?

Clawdeen began picking up speed, trying to outrun her rage. Popped-blister pain was minor compared to the sting of a stab in the back. Her high heels were sinking into the soft earth, and her C cups were in a turbulent state. Pumas and a sports bra would have made a world of difference, but she had been forced into exile the moment she stepped out of the limo. By then the show had already aired, and the RADs were fleeing.

"Couldn't we have packed a bag or two, at least?" Clawdeen asked, risking a mouthful of mosquitoes.

"Couldn't you have *not* gone on TV?" Don fired back. The honor roll student *did* make a good point, as usual.

"I didn't know we were being set up!"

"You *should* have," he grumbled.

"Clawd did it too," Clawdeen added without guilt. Don would never get mad at Clawd—he was the oldest.

"I did it to watch over *you*," he said breathlessly. A star football player, he was better at short sprints than long distances. "To make sure it wasn't a trap."

"And how did that work out?" Howie teased.

Clawd smacked him playfully on the arm. Howie smacked him back.

Clawdeen missed her girls already. *No more gossip sessions, ab-grabbing laughter, clothing swaps, hair-streaking sleepovers, nail-art contests, or professional waxes at the spa.*

She pumped her fists and ran faster. Every twig that snapped beneath Clawdeen's boots was a closed-minded normie. *Banished from our homes. No more Internet. No more television. No more jogging along the river to Blue's bonzer playlists. Forced into hiding. Living in fear.* Clawdeen ran harder. *Snap. Snap. Snap.*

Birds took off in flaps of panic. Rodents dipped back into their holes. Leaves rustled.

The clearing was visible now. Their mother, Harriet, would be there, anxious to guide them to safety.

"Maybe we should grab Mom and go back home," Clawdeen tried. "Maybe it's time we stood up for ourselves instead of being afraid—"

"We're not *afraid*," Howie insisted. "Dad put us in charge of keeping you and Mom safe while he's away, that's all."

Clawdeen rolled her eyes. It was the same story day after day. The boys were supposed to protect the girls. But this girl didn't want protection. She wanted to go back home and confront Cleo. She wanted to check the mail and see if anyone had RSVP'd to her Sassy Sixteen (because what sixteen-year-old wants to be *sweet?*). She wanted to take a long, hot shower.

"You guys stay with Mom, and I'll go back," she pressed.

7

"No. We're a pack," Clawd said, "and—"

"Packs stay together," they all finished, in a mocking tone.

"Keep going. We're almost there," Clawd instructed.

Clawdeen bit her bottom lip and did what she was told. But her tolerance for being babied was wearing as thin as her socks. Forget about protecting *her*—what about their home? Their individual rights? Their *freedom*? Those needed protection way more than she did.

Harriet's athletic silhouette became visible in the distance. As usual, she waved her kids forward, silently urging them to hurry. Going through the motions, Clawdeen picked up her pace, but the flight instinct had yet to kick in. Instead, she wanted to dig in her high heels and fight. And why shouldn't she? She was just weeks away from her sixteenth birthday, too old to follow the pack. It was time to take control of her life, to show her family that she was more than just another shiny coat.

It was time for this Wolf and her L.A.M.B.s to stray.

CHAPTER TWO
FRIGHT OR FLIGHT

Drained and aching from what seemed like hours of sprinting and hiding behind trees, cars, and lampposts, Frankie flopped onto a stone couch in the RADs' underground hideout and surrendered to the weight of her eyelids. As usual, the lair smelled like popcorn and moist earth. The carousel overhead stopped circling at sundown, but familiar voices still swirled all around her. She was not the first to arrive.

Were her parents there? Had they made it safely? Was Brett really to blame for this?

Frankie tried not to think about him or she'd spark. And she couldn't spark. She needed to preserve every last drop of energy in case she had to run again.

Her fingers flopped against the tattered hem of her matronly peasant skirt. It felt frayed and muddy—definitely no longer wearable. She grinned weakly. At least some good had come of this.

"You okay?" Frankie heard a familiar male voice and smelled orange Starburst. She forced her eyes open. No one was there.

"Billy?"

He unhooked a strand of black hair from Frankie's lashes and gently tucked it behind her ear. "Yeah," he said softly.

She struggled to sit up. Her invisible friend gripped her shoulder and eased her back down. "Rest."

Police sirens wailed aboveground. The room became noticeably quieter until they passed.

"I need to apologize," she managed to mumble.

"No one blames you."

Frankie sighed with doubt.

"It's true. You did everything you could to protect us. Everyone knows that. Brett had all of us fooled. Not just you..." Billy kept talking. Going on and on about how Brett was the wrong guy for her. How he had used her to further his film career. How she never should have trusted a normie who wears monster-movie tees.

Frankie nodded in agreement to show Billy she was just as outraged. But if she were being honest, she would have told him that when Brett gave Channel Two the unblurred interviews, he did more than just break her trust. He broke her heart.

The underground lair began filling with the usual, albeit panic-stricken, RADs. Too nervous to sit on the stone club chairs, they paced. Their jittery movements blocked and then unblocked the lanterns that hung from ceiling hooks, creating a dizzying strobe effect. Jackson chewed his bottom lip while his mini fan blew the floppy bangs off his forehead. Beside him Blue peeled off her fingerless gloves and began slathering her scaly skin with Burt's

Bees moisturizer. Deuce removed his green beanie so the snakes on his head could uncoil and stretch. Lala, looking even paler than usual, closed her ruby-red parasol and quickly joined their tight cluster. Julia greeted them with her endearing zombielike stare behind her cat-eye glasses.

Ordinarily, bubbly conversation would fizz from their circle and overflow into the room like shaken soda. But tonight conversation was flat. Instead of giggly gossip, they exchanged *what-do-we-do-now?* glances set to a symphony of nail-biting, toe taps, and muffled sobs.

Billy tugged Frankie's finger. "Let's say hi."

"You go," she said, too embarrassed to face her friends. Not because her mission to liberate the RADs had failed, but because she really liked Brett and had led everyone to believe he liked her too.

Billy squeezed her hand before letting go. "Okay, be right back."

Allowing her eyes to close again, Frankie heard familiar voices wash over her like waves of electricity.

"Who figahd Brett was such a bounce?" Blue said, her Australian accent thicker than usual. "I had him sussed for a real mate."

"Well, thanks to that 'bounce,' I have to go back to Greece," Deuce muttered.

"For how long?" Billy asked.

"Dunno. Long enough for the coach to kick me off the basketball team."

"Does Cleo know yet?" Lala asked.

The sudden *knick-knock knick-knock* of wooden heels and a waft of amber perfume kept Deuce from answering.

"Heyyyy," Cleo trilled, with *meeting-up-for-lattes* flippancy.

"Coooool haaaiiir," Julia droned, noticing Cleo's camera-ready do. The zombie was oblivious to the mounting tension.

Frankie wanted to peek, but opening her eyes had become impossible. She felt as if a dozen chandelier earrings were dangling off her lashes.

"Thanks! I just came from the *Teen Vogue* shoot," Cleo announced. She paused for a second and then asked, "What's wrong with Frankie?"

"She just needs some sleep," Billy insisted. "She'll be fine."

"Really? 'Cause she looks a little green, if you ask me." Cleo giggled.

Frankie's fingertips warmed but didn't spark. If she had a single watt of energy left, she would mummy-wrap the royal *rhymes-with-stitch* so tight that her fake lashes would pop off. *What is she doing here, anyway? She wasn't even in the video.*

"What do *you* want?" Lala asked.

"I came to clear my name," Cleo said, her tone downshifting to serious. "Where's Clawdeen?"

"No one knows." Billy sighed. "She's not answering her phone."

"Anyway, don't you mean *apologize*?" Jackson seethed.

"Cleo *apologize*?" Deuce scoffed. "That'll never happen."

"Exactly, Deucey, because I didn't *do* anything."

"Rubbish!" Blue snapped. "You ruined our lives to impress your new bestie—"

"*Ka!*" Cleo stamped her wooden heel. "Bekka Madden is *not* my bestie!"

"Well, she should be, because we're done," Blue replied.

12

"Will you let me finish?" Cleo asked, hands on hips.

They were silent.

"I admit, I was bitter because you chose the movie over my *Teen Vogue* shoot," Cleo began. "I teamed up with Bekka to erase the video from Brett's computer so it wouldn't air. Not cool, I know. All I wanted was to model with my best friends, so, technically, my heart was in the right place."

Julia hummed in approval.

"But why team up with Bekka?" asked Lala.

"She knew Brett's passwords."

"Why didn't *she* want the movie to air?" asked Jackson.

"Who cares? She had her reasons, but those were mine, okay?"

Frankie's fingertips burned like cheeks blushing. *She* was Bekka's reason.

"Anyway, when I heard Channel Two wasn't going to show the video because of the blurs, I thought everything was golden," Cleo continued. "You guys could model, and I could stop hanging out with Bekka and that pain in the Aswan, Haylee. I had no idea they were going to put it on TV uncensored. I had nothing to do with that! Swearsies on Ra. I was in the Oregon sand dunes fighting for my life in a camel stampede while this was going down. If Melody hadn't filled me in, I never—"

"How *is* Melody? Has anyone talked to her?" Jackson interrupted. "My paranoid mother took my phone."

"Hey, wanna hear something freaky?" Cleo leaned in, ready to dish about the new normie. "Did you know that when she sings—"

Blue cut her off. "Oh, quit your earbashing and stick to the point. Did you throw us under the trolley or not?"

Frankie wished she could have seen Cleo's face. No one *ever* spoke to the royal highness like that.

"Bekka acted alone," Cleo insisted. "The only thing I did wrong was choose a photo shoot over the cause. That's it. I would never put any of you in danger. Not even for *Teen Vogue*. Crown my heart and hope to rot in my tomb." She paused. "Any questions?"

No one said a word. Instead, Frankie heard kissy sounds and *all-is-forgiven* hug purrs.

"Coooooool haaaiiir," Julia droned for the second time.

Cleo giggled. "Thanks, Ghoules."

Wait! I have a question, Frankie thought. *When you said, "Bekka acted alone," did you mean alone without you or alone without Brett? Is Brett innocent? Is—ouch! Tight. Bolt cramp. Ahhhhhhhh...*

Frankie's body began to hum. White-hot currents zipped along her spine and energized her limbs. Her fingers twitched. Her toes wiggled. Her eyes shot open. *Is this how normies feel when they eat sugar?*

Her father was leaning over her and squinting intensely, as if trying to read her thoughts. "How's Daddy's perfect little girl?"

Frankie nodded slowly and sat up. Her mother's warm hands supported her back.

"We were so worried about you," Viktor said. "If Billy hadn't told us where you were..."

"Frankie, another five minutes and you would have been out," Viveka explained. "Memory loss, coma..." She shook the horrible thoughts from her mind.

"Here," Viktor said proudly. A black quilted handbag with bloodred straps dangled from his index finger. "It's for you."

Confused, Frankie looked back at her mother. The bag *was* voltage, but it was an odd time for gifts.

"Go on." Viveka smiled. "Take it."

The lair was teeming with parents racing to embrace their children.

"It's a portable amp machine," Viktor explained. "Keep it close to your body and you'll stay charged."

"We modeled it after a Chanel," Viveka whispered triumphantly.

Frankie turned the bag around in her hands. It buzzed life. The straps were studded with miniature neck bolts, and the interior had more pockets than her Joie cargoes. She instantly transferred her iPhone 4, black-and-green Harajuku Lovers wallet, rhinestone compact, Fierce & Flawless makeup case, pink Lady Gaga key chain, and bag of assorted saltwater taffy from her now-passé silver backpack. Everything fit beautifully.

"I adore it with my entire heart space!" Frankie beamed, pulling her parents into a gigantic thank-you hug. They smelled like chemicals and gardenias—a scent she had come to associate with love.

"A rather unusual time for cutesy adolescent expressions and hugs, wouldn't you agree?" A male voice, deep and melodic, suddenly filled the room.

The Steins pulled apart to find a giant monitor lowering from the ceiling. It stopped in the center of the crowded room and hovered ten feet above the stone floor. The RADs quickly stopped commiserating and focused on the screen, which showed a

15

distinguished man seated under a giant sun umbrella. Wearing mirrored Carrera sunglasses and a gold satin robe, he had a seven-layer tan and slicked-back hair that was stiff with comb tracks. The shot revealed very little about his location, other than the polished wood railing of a yacht. Jay-Z blared in the background. Women giggled. Champagne flutes clinked.

"Forgive us, Mr. D," Viktor said, approaching the screen. "We were just so happy to see that Frankie was safe and—"

Folding his arms across his smooth chest, the man on the monitor shook his head disapprovingly.

"Sorry," Viktor stated humbly.

Three women *click-clack*ed by on-screen wearing heels and the kind of cutout one-pieces that left Mondrian-esque tan lines. Their long pink fingernails raked along the back of Mr. D's neck as they passed.

Embarrassed, Lala buried her face in her palms.

Frankie broke away from her mother and inched toward her friends.

"How'd he get so bronzed?" Cleo asked Lala.

"Thirty hours straight in a tanning bed," she whispered back.

"I hate those things," Frankie interjected, remembering her mortifying electrical surge at the spa. "I felt like I was in a coffin."

Cleo and Lala giggled.

"Um, something tells me he's okay with that," Cleo added.

They giggled again.

Missing the joke, Frankie turned away and whispered into Blue's beach-blond curls, "Who is this guy?"

"Lala's pop," Blue whispered back. "He's the boomer."

"The *what*?"

"The male kangaroo," Blue said.

Frankie knit her brows.

"The boss!"

"Oh."

"Cunning as a dunny rat, he is," Blue continued. "And quite grouse with the sheilas, if you know what I mean."

Frankie nodded like she did.

Mr. D cleared his throat. "I'll save the scolding for another time. I suppose being forced out of your homes is punishment enough for now. Am I right?"

Several parents lowered their heads in shame. Some sniffed back tears. Frankie backed up and hid behind Deuce, just in case Mr. D started looking for a scapegoat. But he didn't seem concerned with blame. Thankfully, no one did. Blame was a luxury they could no longer afford.

"I've made the necessary arrangements," he stated. "My brother Vlad will collect your phones and identification. I have arranged for new mobile devices, phone numbers, and IDs for everyone so you can no longer be traced."

Lala's uncle Vlad appeared before Frankie holding open a giant black sack. No taller than five feet, with a mop of gray hair, round tortoiseshell glasses, and a black-and-white formfitting striped tee, he looked like a Happy Meal–sized Andy Warhol.

"Trick or treat," he said, the tips of his Crest Whitestripped fangs poking his pillowy bottom lip.

Fingers sparking, Frankie searched the crowd for signs of Billy. Her phone had been a gift from him. She couldn't just—

"It's okay," Billy said, as if reading her mind. "I won't take it personally."

Uncle Vlad cocked his head and raised his light eyebrows in a *let's go!* sort of way.

Frankie reached inside her new bag and gripped her phone. Like a happy puppy greeting its master, the phone charged from her touch. Oh, how they would miss each other.

"*Vite, vite!*" urged Uncle Vlad.

Frankie released the phone into the dark sack.

"Wallet too, Sparky."

Not one for being bullied, Frankie considered zapping his pearly fangs into candy corns. But now was not the time to draw attention to herself. Instead, she pulled out her Merston High ID and dropped it into the bag. "The wallet stays with me," she insisted.

"Meowwww," Uncle Vlad mewed. "Feisty Stein has spoken."

Frankie smirked at the nickname; she took it as a compliment. He winked like maybe it was, and then handed her a black envelope.

"What's this?"

"Emergency money, new ID, travel itinerary, and a gift card for a new iPhone redeemable at any Apple Store worldwide."

"Travel itinerary?" Frankie asked. "Where are we going?"

"Make like a librarian and check it out, Feisty." Uncle Vlad gestured toward the roomful of people still waiting for their envelopes. "You're not my only customer."

He and his ominous black sack moved on to Cleo.

"Forget it, mister." She clutched her bag to her chest. "I didn't do anything—I wasn't on TV!"

Frankie rolled her eyes as she pushed her way to the front of the crowd.

"A fleet of jets is currently en route," continued Mr. D. "They will be in the usual spot in three hours. You have been guaranteed safe passage from one of my contacts at the FAA. Remain here until that time. No one is to return home. It's not safe."

Murmurs swelled.

"What's going to happen to Salem when we leave?" asked one of the grown-ups. "Who's going to run my restaurant?"

"And my law practice?"

"And the fire department?"

"What about my students?"

"And my patients?"

The atmosphere quickly shifted from conflict to panic. These were high-powered people, beholden not only to one another but to the entire community. Did Mr. D really expect them to drop everything and leave? Who would take their places? How would society function without them? And what would become of those left behind?

Forgetting her parents' rule about not standing too close to the TV, Frankie approached the monitor and blurted, "Are you sure leaving is the best idea?"

Mr. D leaned closer to the camera, its round eye reflected in his sunglasses. "Ms. Stein?"

Frankie nodded.

He leaned back in his white captain's chair, his fingertips touching. "Yes, I've heard about you."

Frankie beamed. "Thanks."

A few of the grown-ups snickered.

"Sorry, sir," Viktor said, placing his hand on Frankie's shoulder and pulling her back from the screen. "She was just born. What she's trying to say is that some of us are tired of being intimidated. And we want to stay."

"Easy for you to say," snapped Maddy Gorgon, Deuce's mother. "Frankie wasn't in the movie."

"Yes, she *was*," Viveka insisted.

"Just her voice," argued Blue's aunty Coral. "Funny how she conducted her interviews *behind* the scenes. It's like she *knew* this would blow up in our faces."

Frankie felt as if a vacuum hose had been attached to her belly button, the dial set to COMPOSURE SUCK. "We only had one camera!" she snapped. "I guess I could have sat on the subject's lap, or we could have tied it to a pendulum, but—"

Viktor touched Frankie on the shoulder in warning. "Enough," he mumbled.

"That was awesome," Billy whispered in her other ear.

Frankie was too worked up to smile.

"What exactly are you accusing my daughter of?" Viveka asked.

On the screen Mr. D was mumbling his lunch order to a waitress.

"I think you know," Coral said. "That one's been nothing but trouble since the day she was born."

Frankie sparked.

"Hold up a minute, Carol," said Ram de Nile, seated comfortably in a club chair.

20

"It's *Coral*."

"My Cleo wasn't in the movie either," he continued. "Are you suggesting she had an ulterior motive too?"

"Perhaps," Coral pressed.

"Then *I* have a suggestion for *you*," Ram said as Cleo appeared by his side. "Maybe you need to control your niece."

"Rack off!" Blue shouted. "I am in control!"

Lala giggled, and Mr. D turned back to face the group.

"Sounds like it," Ram scoffed.

"Well, I'm not taking any chances," Maddy chimed in. "Deuce and I are going back to Greece."

"What?" Cleo shouted. And then to her boyfriend, "Why didn't you tell me?"

"I just found out an hour ago," he whined.

"How long will he be gone?" Cleo asked Mrs. Gorgon.

"As long as it takes," Maddy said firmly. "Normies all over the world now know who we are. We need to be with family— they're the only ones we can trust."

"That's not true. There are a lot of normies out there who support us," said Jackson, obviously thinking of Melody.

"What about basketball?" Cleo asked. "The coach will kick Deuce off the team if he misses—" She began to cry. "What about *me*?"

"Thanks to your *smart* choices, we're staying right here," Ram declared, even though that's not what Cleo had meant.

Coral waved her black envelope in the air. "Well, Blue is going back to her parents in Bells Beach."

At that, the sea creature broke into salty sobs. The dry scales

21

on her cheeks glistened beneath her tears. Her aunt's hushed promises of daily surf sessions and sunset swims along the Great Barrier Reef brought Blue momentary solace, but then the notion of leaving her friends and missing Clawdeen's Sassy Sixteen tore her up all over again.

"We'll send video of the party," Jackson said, trying to console her.

"Excuse me?" said his mother. "We're not staying."

"*What*? I can't just leave. What about school? My art classes? And *Melody*?"

"She's a sweet girl, Jackson, but the least of my concerns right now."

Fights were breaking out all around Frankie. Parents and kids argued over their futures as Uncle Vlad pried phones from their hands.

Lala was the only one still fixed on the screen. "Does this mean I'm coming to meet you on the yacht, Daddy?" Her voice sweetened with hope.

"La, I'm running an international empire from this boat. It's hardly a Disney cruise," Mr. D explained, in a tone that implied this wasn't the first time he'd said so.

Lala looked down at the fuchsia ribbon laces in her combat boots. After a moment she lifted her moist eyes. "So I'm staying here? With Uncle Vlad?"

Mr. D shook his head.

"Why not?" she asked, burying her pale hands in the sleeves of her boyfriend cardigan. "I'm not like you. I don't show up on camera. No one saw my face."

22

"They know where you live."

"But—"

"You'll have fun in Transylvania," he insisted.

"No." Lala backed away from the screen. "Not the grim-parents, *please*!"

"Stop calling them that. You'll be safe there. If you're lucky, they might even teach you a thing or two about being responsible and taking charge."

Vlad rolled his eyes, taking the dig personally.

"They drink meat shakes and stay inside all day!"

"So, they're a little old-school," admitted Mr. D.

"Dad, when I told Grumpa I wanted to be a veterinarian, he said I already was because I don't eat meat. He doesn't even know the difference between a veterinarian and a vegetarian!"

"They raised me right, didn't they?"

Lala didn't respond.

"Hang in there," Mr. D urged.

"Pun intended," Blue whisper-giggled.

"Grandpa's just teasing you. Give them a chance."

"But, Daddy—"

On-screen, the waitress returned with a sizzling steak on a silver tray.

"I'm afraid I have another meeting," he announced. "Maddy, the phones."

Uncle Vlad emptied the black sack onto the floor. Deuce's fashionably lithe mother stepped forward. "Eyes closed," she called, gripping her black Diors. Everyone closed their eyes and she lifted the sunglasses. The room quickly cooled and then warmed as she lowered the lenses back over her eyes. "All clear," she announced.

Before them sat a stone statue made of their discarded cell phones, wallets, and IDs—another obscure piece of art to clutter their underground hideaway. The latest tribute to their ongoing struggle.

"Good luck to all of you," Mr. D said over the sound of sobs. "And remember, hide with pride."

"Hide with pride," everyone muttered back. Everyone but the Steins.

The screen went black, and the monitor ascended toward the ceiling.

From across the room, Aunty Coral, who was still consoling Blue, fired a round of hate squints at the Steins.

"We should probably get going," Viktor said, placing a protective arm around Frankie's shoulders.

Frankie found it hard to believe her parents were seriously serious about staying. "So that's it? We're just heading back to Radcliffe?"

Viveka knelt down and took her daughter's hand. "That's it," her violet eyes steady and sure. "We've been doing it our way for centuries, and it hasn't gotten us very far. So now we'll try it your way."

"*My* way?" Frankie sparked and then pulled back her hand. Imagining herself the leader of a successful revolution felt more uplifting than underwire. But spoken aloud, those words were heavy, weighted down with responsibility and consequence. And after her many failed attempts as a freedom fighter, she questioned her ability to carry that burden alone. "It's not like I have a plan or anything."

"Good." Viktor snickered, obviously thinking of her track record too. "Because right now all we need to do is stay put and stay safe. Our goal is to continue living our lives. Business as usual. That's it. Nothing else. Not yet. No plots, no plans, no schemes. Not until we know what and whom we're dealing with. Got it?"

"Got it," Frankie agreed, even though she didn't. Not completely. But she would. As soon as she found Brett at school on Monday and asked—no, *demanded*—that he cop to his role in this mess. Then, once she'd dealt with him accordingly, she'd agree to her father's rule.

Amid tearful good-byes and a few vengeful glances, Viktor led his family toward the old wooden door. Along the way Frankie and Viveka broke off to hug friends and wish them well.

"You're really staying?" asked Ms. J, reaching under her thick black glasses and dabbing the corner of her eye with a balled-up tissue.

"We are," Viveka said, grinning at Frankie. Frankie grinned back.

"I wish Jackson and I could, but—"

"With all due respect, Viv," said Maddy Gorgon, cutting Ms. J off. "Do you really think staying is in the best interest of your daughter?"

"Absolutely," Viveka said, her certainty reflected in the lenses of Maddy's Diors.

"It was my idea," Frankie said, rushing to her mother's defense.

"We've learned a lot from her over the last few months." Viveka beamed at her daughter.

"Our kids are clever. No question about that." Maddy cupped the back of her yellow-and-green head scarf. "But in times like these, I think it's wise to let the grown-ups do the teaching."

"We're teaching her about life," said Viveka. And then to Frankie she added, "And she's teaching us about living."

"Well then," said Maddy with a caustic grin. "Let's hope she knows what she's doing."

Ms. J sniffed. "You'd better take good care of yourselves. We want you here in one piece in case we come back."

In case? Frankie had never considered that these people might be gone for good. She had been too consumed with her heartache. Too preoccupied with confronting Brett. Too fixated on her parents' voltage decision to stay.

Ashamed by her thoughtlessness, Frankie adjusted her inner empathy dial and tuned in to the frequency of the room. Sorrow hovered, gray and oppressive as Salem fog.

Parents had formed clusters, discussing their barely baked plans in hushed tones. Jackson sat in a club chair, leaning forward as if trying not to puke. Lala and Blue giggle-sobbed as they recorded video messages on each other's phones. Cleo's gold-wrapped arms encircled Deuce. Soaked false lashes dangled from her eyes like branches trapped at the mouth of a waterfall. If tear salt could calcify, it would have hung from her lids like stalactites. Could this really be good-bye forever?

Frankie couldn't imagine school without these people. And she couldn't imagine them without each other. Now, more than ever, she was determined to make things right. To be the one associated with uniting instead of dividing. To bring meaning to her life and to feel worthy of being called "Daddy's perfect little girl." She owed it to her friends, her parents, and her future.

Like Martin Luther King Jr., Frankie dreamed of living in a nation where people would not be judged by the color of their skin but by the content of their character. The sooner she realized that dream, the sooner she could get started on Katy Perry's and live the teenage one.

CHAPTER THREE
UNDER THE INFLUENCE

The front door of the Carver house blew open with urgency. Melody lifted her throbbing head off the kitchen table and braced herself for a follow-up slam that never came.

"Hullo?" her older sister, Candace, called out, spitting a pistachio shell across the table at Melody.

No one answered.

The girls exchanged a terrified glance that seemed to ask, *Are we about to be taken into custody? Questioned for our involvement in "The Ghoul Next Door"? Kidnapped and tortured until we reveal the RADs' hiding places?*

If only they knew.

"We have fully loaded snipers, you know!" Candace added.

Melody rolled her eyes. "The sniper is the shooter, not the weapon," she whispered.

Candace shrugged in her typical *I-should-get-points-for-even-*

*knowing-that-word-because-perfectly-symmetrical-blonds-
like-me-aren't-expected-to-and-I-did* sort of way.

"Where is she?" cried the intruder.

The familiar high-heeled stabs of Tory Burch hiking boots
pocking the wood floors put them at ease.

"Hi, Mom…" Candace muttered, cracking into another
pistachio.

Melody hit REDIAL on her cell phone for what felt like the zil-
lionth time that night. Once again it went straight to voice mail.
She hung up. "I'm telling you, something isn't right with Jackson."

Glory Carver appeared in the doorway of the woodsy kitchen.
Her petite frame was wrapped in an unassuming black trench
coat, allowing her auburn curls to take center stage. "Where's
your father? He should have been home hours ago."

Melody shrugged. "I dunno."

"Oh well, I can't wait another minute. Let's hear it," Glory
insisted, rubbing her hands together anxiously.

Melody's stomach dipped. There was nothing about this
nightmare she wanted to share, especially with *her*.

"Come on, I didn't race home from book club to be stared
at. Go!"

"Aren't you going to close the front door?" Melody asked,
unable to look her mother in the eye.

"Really? The *door*?" Glory untied her trench and joined her
daughters at the table—a glass oval that mocked their rustic
home with its *I'm-from-Beverly-Hills* shine. "That's all?"

"Yup." Melody got up and yanked open the wood-paneled
fridge. The cool air was soothing.

"Why so morose?" Glory asked.

Melody rolled her eyes at the organic fat-free milk.

"Mom, I think the expression is *sow more oats*," Candace said, enunciating carefully. "And I agree. She is totally obsessing over Jackson. Sister needs to date."

"Actually," Glory said, giggling, "I meant *morose*." She fixed her green eyes on Melody. "I don't understand."

"Lots of reasons." Melody shut the fridge and stomped off to slam the front door shut. *Could it be that my friends have become the target of a massive monster hunt?* she wanted to yell. *Or that my boyfriend hasn't picked up his phone in three hours? Oh no, wait! I know why I'm being so morose. It's because Cleo's butler, Manu, gave me reason to believe that you're not my real mother!* But genealogy was not the priority. Finding Jackson was. So Melody walked back into the kitchen without saying a word.

"I just assumed you'd be celebrating, that's all," Glory explained with a self-pitying shrug.

"Celebrating?" Melody asked, confused.

"Your sister texted the good news from the *Teen Vogue* shoot."

"Good news?"

"When I heard you got your singing voice back, I nearly jumped out of my J Brands!"

Candace cracked another pistachio.

"Wait." Melody leaned against the counter and stuffed her hands into the pockets of her hoodie. "You're talking about my singing?"

Glory nodded. "Of course. I want to hear it." She slapped her hands together as if in prayer and mouthed, *Ohpleaseohpleaseoh-*

please. "Do 'Defying Gravity' from *Wicked*. Just like you used to. That was always my favorite."

Candace burst out laughing.

"Mom, I'm not in the mood right—"

"Babe!" Beau called as he entered the house. "You're never going to believe it!"

"I know! She got her voice back!" Glory raced to the foyer to greet him. "It's eight thirty; where have you been?"

"The phones at the office have been ringing like mad."

Perma-tanned and dressed in an Armani suit, the age-defying plastic surgeon entered the kitchen. Loosening his tie, he kissed each of his daughters on the forehead and then lowered himself into one of the black open-hand-shaped chairs around the table. Glory popped his favorite Lean Cuisine meal—Baja-style quesadilla—into the microwave and set the timer. "Why didn't you let the service answer?"

"Morbid curiosity," he said. "The calls were from teenagers asking if we could give them fangs, horns, tails...you name it. They wanted to look like..." He snapped his fingers, trying to remember the word, then gave up and moved on. "Anyway, at first Dr. Kramer and I thought it was just another practical joke, like the one those Merston kids pulled on that poor guy Brett. But then we heard about the show on Channel Two and—"

"NUDI power!" Candace shouted, punching her fist in the air.

"What's a NUDI?" Glory asked over the beeping microwave.

"Normies Uncool with Discriminating Idiots," Candace explained. "Melly, it's working. Normies want to be RADs! Our message is totally getting through!" She began texting Billy. "Man, this is gonna look great on my college applications."

"That's it! That's what they're called—RADs!" Beau said, fanning his steaming quesadilla. "And from what I understand, some of them live on our street!" He sipped some wine that had appeared in front of him thanks to Glory. "Dr. Kramer is dying to spot one, so I invited his family over for dinner on Sunday night. They have two kids your age, so—"

"So *what*? You're starting up a side business now?" Melody snapped. "Come see the weirdos on Radcliffe Way! Dinner included in the cost of admission! Free hunting nets while supplies last."

"What's wrong with *you*?" he asked.

"So morose," Candace explained. "But she's right, Dad. They're not circus freaks."

Melody nodded in agreement.

"I never said they were—"

"By the way, are the Kramer kids boys or girls?"

"Girls."

"Candace out."

"Not a chance," Beau insisted. "Attendance is mandatory."

"Beau, why did you invite people over the night before our vacation?" Glory asked, filling his wineglass. "We have to leave the next morning."

"It was the only night they could do it."

"Pathetic," Melody mumbled under her breath. Were her parents really being this flip in the face of something so serious? Did the bad news have to happen to *them* to make them care? Wasn't it enough that it was happening to their neighbors?

"But we're going to be packing and—"

"Don't worry," Beau said, lifting his glass by the stem. "I'll get takeout from the Hideout Inn, you'll put it in a Pyrex dish, and they'll think you made it."

Glory smiled and slapped her husband five. "I knew there was a reason I married you."

Do you actually hear yourselves? Melody was about to shout. But her iPhone started to ring.

Jackson!

Hurrying to pick it up, she couldn't help wondering how involved she would be in "the cause" if her boyfriend weren't a victim. Or how concerned Candace would be if she didn't think "NUDI Leader" would look good on her college applications. But Melody dismissed those thoughts, wanting to believe she'd care more than her parents. A lot more.

"Hello?" she blurted, even though the call was coming from a blocked number.

A voice whispered on the other end. "Melody, it's Sydney Jekyll. I mean, Ms. J. Your biology teacher. Jackson's mother."

Melody's mouth dried. "Is he okay?"

"He's fine." Ms. J sighed. "He just refuses to leave without saying good-bye."

"*Leave?* Where is he going?" A cyclone of nausea tore through her.

Who is it? mouthed Glory.

Melody dismissed her with a wave and hurried for the privacy of the living room.

"Can you be at Crystal's Coffee across from McNary Field Airport in forty minutes?"

33

"Uh-huh," Melody managed.

"Good. See you soon. And make sure no one is following you."

The line went dead.

Melody checked the side-view mirror one last time—nothing but darkness and streetlights behind them.

"This is it," she whispered, spotting the only three illuminated letters on the coffee shop's marquee. "Left at the '*fee*.'"

"Ha!" Candace said to the decrepit sign. "You think Frankie could make that light back up with her hands?"

Melody didn't know. And she wasn't in the mood to guess.

Candace flicked on her turn signal. "Let's do this!" As she turned the wheel sharply, the BMW screeched into the Crystal's Coffee lot.

She parked next to a Tacoma with a window made of duct tape and cardboard. Melody slumped down in her seat. "At least turn off the lights."

"Okay, you really need to relax," Candace snapped, obviously tired of Melody's nonstop paranoia.

"Tell that to your outfit."

Candace looked down and giggled. Dressed in Glory's camouflage bird-watching vest and trucker hat with binoculars around her neck and a warbling whistle poking out of the pocket, she was hard to take seriously. But her sister was right. Candace did need to relax. At least about being followed.

"I don't see their car. Do you think we missed them? Or what if—" Melody couldn't bear to finish the thought. It was one thing if Jackson had left, quite another if he'd been taken.

"Haven't you ever had to ditch a stalker?"

Melody shook her head.

"People who are in hiding don't park in plain view."

"True," Melody admitted, eyeing the dilapidated roadside diner. The shutters were drawn. "What would you do? You know, if your boyfriend was leaving?" Saying the words out loud made her insides squinch up, like being zipped into a jacket several sizes too small.

"And I wasn't already bored with him?"

"Obviously!"

"Hmmm." Candace tapped her chin. "That's never actually happened. But I guess I'd make him stay."

"How?"

"That's your job." Candace leaned over and patted Melody on the shoulder. "Mine is to keep watch on stakeout duty." She pulled the bird whistle from her pocket and blew. It sounded like a woodpecker that had swallowed a squeaky toy. "When you hear that, it means 'get out as fast as you can.' Now go before he leaves."

Leaves? Melody's chest zipped even tighter.

Rigged with bells, the door chimed as she opened it. Not even the sweet coffee-and-doughnuts smell could stir her appetite. The Formica counter, silver-and-black stools, and five red booths were predictable. The score of *La Bohème* playing on the jukebox, not so much. Was this really the last place she and Jackson would ever kiss? As she stepped inside, Melody flipped her hoodie over her head. It was the closest thing she had to a hug.

35

There were only two customers: a balding man in a corduroy blazer hunched over a plate of spaghetti, and a black-haired boy immersed in a copy of *Hot Rod* magazine. He had a scar across his cheek and wore a T-shirt that said HELLO, MY NAME IS RICK. Melody's forehead began to panic-sweat. Jackson was already gone.

"Table for one?" asked the overbleached blond waitress with a snap of her minty gum. Her age-spotted hands hovered over a stack of menus.

"Ummm," Melody stalled. *Now what? Go back to the car? Wait? Show the waitress a picture of Jackson? Or maybe D.J.? Ask if she saw one of them?* Melody was bombarded with options, yet none of them seemed worth considering. *He was supposed to be here!* "Actually, I'm meeting—"

Ping!

Melody quickly checked her phone.

TO: MC

oct 14, 9:44 PM

BLOCKED: SIT WITH RICK.

She lifted her gaze. Rick lowered his magazine and tried to smile, but a quivering pout was the best he could do.

Yes!

"I'm going to sit with that guy."

The waitress winked in an *I-would-too-if-I-were-twenty-years-younger* sort of way.

Up close, there was no mistaking the crackle in Jackson's hazel eyes. But the black hair? The scar? The *Hot Rod* mag? And where were his glasses?

"Wait," Melody said, sliding into the booth beside him. There were two plates on the table: an untouched slice of Oreo cookie cheesecake and a side salad. "D.J.?"

"No, it's *me*," Jackson said, managing to conceal everything but his kind voice. "I'm in disguise mode. Do I make a good bad boy?"

"The waitress thought you were cute." Melody tried to sound upbeat. She reached for his hand and held it to her face, wanting—no, needing—to inhale the familiar waxy scent of his pastel crayon–smudged fingers. But the colors had been replaced with harsh black stains. Hair dye. And now they smelled like public-bathroom soap and coarse paper towels.

"How was the *Teen Vogue* shoot?" he asked, as if it were any other day.

Melody tried pretending that it was. "Cleo and I kind of bonded, so that was good. I got my singing voice back and performed for three camels named Niles, Humphrey, and Luxor. And this guy, Manu, gave me very good reason to think some woman named Marina is my real mother."

Jackson pushed the cheesecake aside. "I find that hard to believe."

"Which part?"

"All of it."

"Believe it," Melody said, before sharing the details.

"Did you ask your mom about it?" Jackson asked.

Melody shook her head.

"Why not?"

"Because I was too busy wondering if you were alive." Which was mostly true. But there was a part of Melody that wasn't ready for that conversation. The part that didn't know how she'd react if Manu was right. Tears rushed to her eyes. "You're not *really* leaving, are you?"

Nodding, Jackson hooked the hood of her sweatshirt and pulled her close. Their foreheads touched. "Tonight," he mumbled. "London. On a private jet. I don't know for how long." He paused. "I hate this."

The tears began to fall. Hot and fast, they slithered down Melody's cheeks and off her jaw.

She pulled back and looked Jackson in the eye. "Can't you tell your mom you want to stay? You could wear this disguise. Switch schools. No one would ever know."

"I tried. A hundred times, at least. She told me not to bring it up anymore. I promised I wouldn't if she promised to get you here."

"Well, try *again*," Melody insisted, wondering if that's what Candace had meant by *make him stay*.

"Fine," he agreed, with surprising ease. He lifted his eyes to meet hers. "One condition: You have to stick around while I talk to her."

"Why?"

Jackson half-smiled. "Because if she has as much trouble saying no to you as I do, then the flight is as good as canceled."

Riding the updraft of possibility, Melody leaned in to kiss him.

"What's this about a canceled flight?"

She quickly pulled away.

38

Ms. J was hovering above them, her shiny black bob swinging across her jaw. Her signature matte red lipstick had been freshly applied.

"Nothing," Jackson assured her. "Everything is still on schedule."

"Good." She slid across the open seat and looked at the wooden bowl of iceberg lettuce as if it were some kind of insult. "I know I promised you alone time, but one more second in that bathroom and I would have contracted the hantavirus."

Melody grinned like she completely understood. It was something she found herself doing often with her boyfriend's-mom-slash-beyond-intellectual-biology-teacher.

"Go ahead, ask her," Jackson whispered, nudging Melody.

"You," she whispered back.

"Ask me what?" Ms. J asked while signaling the waitress for the check. "This had better not be about staying, because—"

"You can't leave," Melody blurted.

Ms. J began blinking, as if genuinely interested in what Melody had to say. "Explain."

"Um, I just think that..." Melody stammered, the way she often did in class when called on for an answer she didn't know. But she *did* know this answer. It was Ms. J's willingness to hear it that she hadn't expected.

"You're a teacher..." she began, thinking it best not to center her plea on broken teenage hearts. The woman was a scientist. A rational thinker. She would, therefore, require a rational argument. "And a role model. Not only for RADs, but for normies too."

Ms. J nodded in agreement. Melody could feel Jackson grinning beside her.

"If you leave, it sends a message that when the going gets tough, the tough *leave*, and—"

The waitress slid the check onto the table, but Ms. J's focus remained fixed on Melody. "What about the safety of my son?"

"Mom, I can—"

Melody gripped his thigh, squeezing him silent. "Keep Jackson in this disguise. Send him to another school. Hide with pride. Isn't that your motto? But you need to stay at Merston and be an advocate for the RADs who are still here." Melody leaned across the table and whispered in Ms. J's ear. "And show Jackson that his mother isn't afraid to fight."

Ms. J pulled off her Woody Allen–esque glasses and rubbed her eyes.

Jackson and Melody held hands under the table, their grip tightening with every passing second.

Putting on her glasses, Ms. J turned to her son and said, "You would have to go into hiding."

"That's fine."

"Which means no one, and I mean *no one*"—she paused to glare at Melody—"can know where you are."

"Fine," they answered together. At least they'd be in the same time zone.

Ms. J slapped down a black American Express credit card issued to someone named Rebecca Rose, peeled the protective plastic off a new iPhone, and then began texting.

Jackson pulled his hand away. "What are you doing?"

"Texting the flight crew about my vegan meal."

Melody's heart sank. "But I thought—"

Ms. J placed her phone on the paper place mat and met their eyes. "You thought *what*? That I would let a perfectly good tofu lasagna go to waste?"

"Huh?" Melody asked.

"I told them to put it in a to-go box. We'll have to swing by the tarmac so we can pick it up." She pushed her salad aside. "I'm starving. And it's going to be a long night."

Melody and Jackson exchanged a victorious hug while Ms. J signed the check. *Make out for hours* ranked number one on Melody's what-to-do-next list. Instead, she stuck to her word, wished them both luck, and hurried off to meet Candace.

Nothing about the parking lot had changed, and yet everything about it looked different. The half-lit coffee sign suddenly seemed charming. The duct-taped car was no longer pathetic; it was a survivor. And Candace wasn't mocking Melody's paranoia with her bird-watching costume—she was being supportive. All because Jackson was staying. And regardless of the promise they had made to Ms. J, he would find a way to stay in touch.

He always did.

CHAPTER FOUR
PACK MEN

As she'd suspected, the sudsy nest of hair and soap chips still clogged the shower drain. The hot water didn't shrink the clump as Clawdeen had hoped. Now, ankle deep in boy scum, she would have to reach into the tepid slough to remove the blockage—something she refused to do without a Hazmat suit. This situation made her miss the comforts of home, and her girly bathroom, even more.

Two nights at the Hideout Inn—the family-owned restaurant and inn that encouraged guests to "unplug" with a strict no-TV-or-Internet policy—was a new record. Until now the Wolfs had spent the night only during their full-moon transitions. They posted a SORRY, ALL FULL sign, locked the doors, drew the blinds, and feasted. Stays maxed out at twenty-four hours. The instant they switched back to normalish, the pack returned to Radcliffe Way, and the inn reopened to the public.

Closing for any amount of time put a strain on their finances, since the steakhouse had been rated among the top ten restaurants in Salem for the past six years.

But this time, the strain was on Clawdeen's sanity. If she had to spend one more day sharing a bathroom with her brothers, she'd—

"Ahhhh!" A gallon of ice-cold water splashed over her head.

"Dinner's ready!" announced Don, dropping a plastic milk jug onto the tiled floor. It landed with a hollow bounce. Howie burst out laughing, and then the two triplets took off, slamming the door behind them.

Shivering and disgusted, Clawdeen shut off the faucet. "You're going to pay for this, Cleo," she muttered, holding her ex-friend responsible as she sidestepped anthills of stubble, clipped nails, and discarded underwear. Appetite-suppressing odors clung to her hair—a condition the perpetually upright toilet seat only made worse. If her friends could see her now...what would they laugh at first? Her matted curls? Chipped nails? The ill-fitting brown HIDEOUT INN souvenir T-shirt from the gift shop? Probably the shirt. But what was she supposed to do? Her clothes were back home...along with her makeup, her privacy, and her life.

Downstairs in the restaurant, everything but the full moon was present and accounted for. The red velvet curtains, which Clawdeen had helped her mother make back when they first opened for business, kept the parking lot from view, giving guests the illusion that they were nestled inside a cozy dining room in the Alps, not a mere ten miles north of Salem just off the freeway. Candles flickered inside sangria-colored votives. The tepee of logs in the stone fireplace was ablaze. Eighteen tables were set but unoccupied. Mom was in the kitchen heating up another batch of rolls. The guys were already eating, seated around a central circular table, deep in conversation and second helpings.

"Hi, Deenie." Her father's serious expression quickly melted into one of sticky sweetness. "How's my precious little pup?"

"Hey, Dad," she said, kissing the top of his head before sitting. Clawrk Wolf's lush black hair and thick eyebrows always made her think of Seth's father from *The O.C.* "Do you think we can work on my driving this week? Two more weeks until I'm sixteen."

"When I get back," he said. "I'm leaving for a construction job in Beaverton tomorrow. I'll be gone until Thursday."

"Anything good?" she asked, hoping for more industrial head nails, metal gates, or marble chunks. Or possibly something unexpected, like the mannequins from that old department store he'd demolished. Not that it really mattered. As long as she could DIY his trash into treasure, her video blog—Where There's a Wolf, There's a Way—would keep gaining followers. Her first episode, called "Lip Glass"—in which she'd mounted glass panes on her wall and covered them with colorful lipstick kisses from all her friends—had already brought in seven followers. Before long she'd be fielding calls for her own show on the DIY Network. Then she'd move out, buy a massive New York–style loft, DIY it diva-style, and invite all of her friends (including Anya the waxer) to move in. From that moment on, the only fur lying around would be the fabulous faux kind.

"I'm building a kids' tree house and jungle gym in some hoity-toity couple's backyard," he explained, spooning a mound of sautéed mushrooms onto his plate. "So probably a ton of wood chips."

"Perfect." Clawdeen smiled, thinking of how she could experiment with new nail-art designs on the wood chips and then glue them to the outside of her laptop. How blog-able was that?

"Boys," Clawrk said, chewing, "I'm counting on you to keep your mom and Deenie safe while I'm gone." He sighed. "At least Leena is safe at Arrowhead."

"Wish we could say the same about her roommates," Don joked.

The other boys laughed.

"If you really cared about safety, you guys would clean the pit hairs out of the soap and unclog the drain," Clawdeen said, even though she knew that wasn't what her father meant. She was tired of being overprotected and underestimated, especially by a pack of boys who didn't know how much was too much when it came to squeezing a tube of toothpaste. "I don't understand why we have to share one bathroom when we have the entire inn to ourselves," she continued.

Overcome by the rich aroma of warm butter and beef, she quickly stabbed the last New York strip with her fork and dropped it onto her plate, beating Clawd by a millisecond.

"Because I want to keep this place clean," Harriet called from the kitchen.

"She's right," said Clawrk. "We need to be ready for guests the instant that ALL FULL sign comes down."

"*Baaaaap!*" Nino burped. The boys howled. "I don't have an

ALL FULL sign, because I love Mom's steak," he added, swiping the hair from his eyes.

"You're not the only one, son. Normies go crazy when they can't get a reservation. They're addicted to your mother's cooking." Clawrk glanced around the empty dining room. "That movie was bad for business. Very bad."

"Why?" Rocks chewed loudly. "The Hideout wasn't even in the movie."

Clawdeen rolled her eyes. "He means because we have to hide here, so the place is closed."

Rocks stared at her blankly.

"No money!" she explained.

"Yeah," scoffed Howie. "I wonder whose fault *that* is."

Clawdeen quickly flashed her brother a mouthful of chewed meat.

"If you're not going to finish that, I will," Nino offered.

"Ew!" Clawdeen giggled.

"So, Dad," Clawd said, "remember I told you football scouts were coming to Merston? Well, Coach Donnelly texted. They'll be there on Monday."

Clawrk cracked open a beer and took a long swig.

"Coach saw the video and knows I'm a RAD and all, but he's cool with it," Clawd went on. "He even said he'll drive me back after the game. And if I want that scholarship—"

Clawrk slammed down his beer. "You didn't tell him where we are, did you?"

"Course not. But even if I did, it'd be fine. He's cool."

"Does he know the inn is ours? Or that Charlie and Joanne Stewart are made-up owners?"

46

"No, I swear," Clawd insisted. "I've never told anyone that. And I never would."

"I read that people are hunting us for rewards," Howie announced.

"You *read*?" Clawdeen teased.

"How much are they asking for you?" he wondered.

"You couldn't afford it, bro."

"That's what you think." Howie reached into the pocket of his jeans and flicked a nickel at Don. "Keep the change."

Everyone laughed except their dad, who was considering Clawd's request, and Clawd, who was waiting to hear his fate.

"I'll need to talk to the coach."

"Sure," Clawd said, offering his phone.

"And you'll take the car. I don't want him knowing we're here." Clawd nodded.

Clawrk looked toward the kitchen, as if consulting his wife. Rolling up the sleeves of his stained white thermal, he leaned back in his chair and announced, "As long as you knock the socks off those scouts! And take that girly earring out of your ear."

"*Promise!*" Clawd leaned across the table and high-fived his father. His brothers howled their support.

"I think I'll go with you," Clawdeen said casually. "I can check the mail for RSVPs, get some fresh clothes, check in with some friends, you know—"

"You don't think you're still having that Sweet Sixteen party, do you?" asked Howie in his usual know-it-all way.

"*Sassy* Sixteen. And why not?" She tried dodging them. "It's two weeks away. This will all be over by then."

47

"Yeah, right." Howie shook his head in disbelief. "Who told you that? The other minorities on this planet?"

"Maybe," Clawdeen said.

"You mean the ones who have been fighting for equal rights for, I dunno, about five *thousand* years?"

The other brothers snickered.

"Yeah, I bet they're working overtime to have this whole racism thing wrapped up by your Sweet—I mean your *Sassy*—Sixteen."

"That's enough!" snapped Clawrk, coming to his daughter's rescue.

"Thank you, Daddy," Clawdeen cooed. "I was just hoping to check on the house and pick up a few things. It's not like I'm going to school or anything."

"No way," her dad said. "You're staying here with your brothers, where it's safe."

What? Why? Frustration formed in the pit of Clawdeen's stomach. Gathering strength, it swirled toward her heart and up through her throat. If she let it out, it would sound like, *What a massive double standard! This is so unfair! I'm running away to live with the Kardashians!*

But it was clear from the dark circles under her father's eyes, his rounded shoulders, and his shredded fingernails that this was a bad time to fight for equal rights. Knowing he would be away on a construction job and unable to protect them was obviously stressing him out big-time. Why make things worse? Instead, Clawdeen wiped her mouth on a napkin like a good little girl. Just like everyone expected her to.

Later that night, she woke to the sound of wheels crunching over gravel. Confused by gauzy remnants of sleep, she tried to place her surroundings. Darkness. Blankets that smelled like wet dog instead of breezy-clean fabric softener. This was definitely not her bedroom on Radcliffe Way.

Something began to rustle, like a body squirming against a leather seat. It was breathing. Clawdeen's heartbeat began to accelerate. Adrenaline pumped her awake.

Oof! A shoe slammed on top of her ribs. A second one quickly followed. Then something lighter. She bit her lower lip and refused to move.

"I know you're back there," said Clawd.

Oops.

Clawdeen bicycle-kicked the stinky blanket off her body. "How?" she asked, hoisting herself off the car floor and onto the backseat.

"You started snoring the minute we hit the highway."

"And you let me stay?" she asked, never failing to be surprised by her older brother. "What if Dad finds out?"

"I'll say I didn't know you were here."

"What if something happens to me?" she teased.

He turned around to face her. "I won't let it."

"Why are you doing this?"

"Because I know sometimes they don't treat you fairly," Clawd admitted.

Clawdeen smiled. *Finally, someone understands.*

"What are Mom and Dad going to say when they wake up and you're gone?" Clawd tested her.

"Dad is taking off for Beaverton at, like, four in the morning, and Mom is driving to the Seattle Marketplace to stock up on food. She leaves before we wake up and won't be home until Monday after dinner. As long as we head back after your game, we'll beat her."

"And the brothers?"

"You slipped a note under their door promising to buy them a Wii for Christmas if they keep quiet."

"I did?"

Clawdeen giggled. "Don't worry, I'll pay you back as soon as my DIY show takes off. Now can we please get out of this car and go home? I'm going to start shedding if I don't take off these gift shop clothes."

"Wait! We have to be careful," Clawd insisted, opening the door. "I parked three blocks from the house to avoid suspicion. Let's take the ravine."

"The streets are better. People will be looking for us in the ravine. But if we just walk normally, no one will suspect a thing."

"That's ridiculous. We're just asking to get caught." Clawd gently shut the door.

Clawdeen opened hers. "No. If we take the ravine, we're asking to get caught."

"My road trip, my plan," Clawd insisted.

"Forget it. You go your way, and I'll go mine." Clawdeen wasn't sure what she was fighting for anymore, but she refused to back down.

"I'm not just going to leave you," he huffed.

50

"Then come with me on the street," Clawdeen said, stepping onto the curb.

She began walking down Glacier Road feeling naked and exposed. Alive and in charge. Afraid and energized. Indisputably independent. She liked it.

"Wait!" whispered Clawd, scrambling to catch up.

They walked half the block in silence, senses attuned, hackles up.

Her brother finally broke the silence. "Why are you always trying to be the alpha?"

"I'm not *trying*," Clawdeen whispered. "I am."

"Very funny." Clawd chuckled.

But somehow, someday, Clawdeen would find a way to prove it. And once she did, the last laugh would be hers.

If they could see me now…

Billy imagined the Richter levels of envy that would quake through the guys at school if they knew he was spending his Sunday naked in Candace Carver's bedroom. And that it smelled like gardenia, vanilla, and hot girl. Not that he would ever brag. That was *très* déclassé. Besides, it wasn't even like that. He and Candace would have preferred to hang at Whole Latte Love, but there were only so many times (fourteen and counting) they could crack up at the *invisible-boy-sneaking-bites-of-people's-scones* routine before wanting to have an actual conversation. And Candace said she didn't want people to think she was talking to herself. But she had been doing exactly that for the past twenty minutes, anyway, so what was the big deal? But, hey, if Billy understood the opposite sex, he wouldn't have spent the entire night journaling about—

"...are you even listening?" Candace snapped, pacing back and forth in front of her frilly pink girl bed. "Wait, you didn't leave, did you?" She splayed her arms as if feeling her way around in a dark closet. *"Billy?"*

It was the perfect opportunity to tie the laces of her brown riding boots together, but pranks were for the lighthearted, and he was feeling anything but.

"I'm still here," he said, pacing alongside her. Curling up on the canopy bed would have been preferable but impolite, considering his bare-bottomed state.

"Oh, good," Candace said, then continued her story. "So, Ali thinks I should give her my ticket now that she and Vanessa made up, because she claims it was bought for her and only given to me to make her jealous, which, by the way, Danice says is total BS, because she was there when Vanessa was making her Evite list. So now Ali is giving *me* attitude, when this is really about her and Vanessa...I think. Nate Garrett says she's just threatened because I'm a three-temperature girl—hot, cool, and warm—and she's just plain frigid. Which, by the way, I told her. And now she's really pissed at me. Not that I care. She's the one who said RADs should have their own school. I told you that, right? I mean, it doesn't get more un-NUDI than that. So I say see ya later, Ali-hater..."

"Good for you," Billy said, distracted. It wasn't that he didn't care about Candace's latest drama. Or that he didn't appreciate her mischievous sense of humor, trendsetting style, or blond-haired, blue-eyed magnificence. Because he did. He adored their budding friends-without-benefits relationship; wouldn't have had it any other way. His mind was just somewhere else. Which made concentrating feel like riding a bucking bronco. After a second or two, he was thrown.

"Your turn," Candace said, sitting on the edge of her bed, crossing her gray legging-clad legs under her ivory slip dress. "I'm listening," she said, cocking her head.

"What?" Billy asked defensively.

"Do you seriously think I made up that story about Ali just to hear myself talk?"

"Huh?"

"You're obviously bummed about something. You haven't done one funny thing since you got here." She grinned, pleased with her detective work. Anyone else would have seemed smug. But Candace radiated eighteen-karat charm. "I opened with an emotional crisis; now it's your turn."

"No fair! Yours was fake." He finally smiled.

She sighed, shaking her head like a disappointed guidance counselor. "It's Frankie, isn't it?"

The mention of her name turned a winch in Billy's stomach. "Now that Brett's out of the picture, I thought maybe I'd have a chance."

"Yayyyy!" Candace kicked her legs. "Fix-up time!"

"No," Billy said, knocking his head against the pewter rod of her canopy bed. "That's the problem. She's not going to want me, for the same reasons you didn't want to meet at Whole Latte Love."

Candace opened her mouth to protest but stopped herself. He was right. Not even she could argue with that.

"I'm not even registered at Merston," he admitted for the first time. "Ms. J is the only teacher who knows I exist. I just go to hang out with you guys and learn."

"But Frankie knows you exist," Candace tried. "You're one of her closest f—"

"Don't say it," he insisted, dreading the *F*-word. Being her *friend* was like using a spoon to cut steak. It scratched the surface but would never go deep. "It doesn't matter, anyway. She deserves more than a guy who can't wear clothes."

"Why?" Candace asked.

"Because she's a respectable girl who—"

"No." Candace giggled. "Why don't you wear clothes?"

The question startled Billy. It had been six years since someone asked him that. Even longer since he'd asked himself.

When he first started disappearing, strategically placed garments were enough to conceal his missing parts. A glove on the invisible hand. A Band-Aid over a clear eyebrow. A scarf wrapped around a see-through neck. But the holes eventually spread, expanding and connecting like puddles, until everything was covered. At that point, fading out seemed like the only option.

But that was before his parents introduced him to the

alliance. Before he met the others. Before he knew Frankie. Before Candace reminded him that he had options.

"I guess I could wear clothes if I wanted to," he mused. "But what about my face, my hair, my..."

"*My gawd*, Billy! This depressing town has one season: overcast! And yet check out my arms." She held them out. They were the color of peanut butter. "Looks like I just made out with the sun, doesn't it?"

He nodded.

"It's called a spray tan. My dad's hair is black, not gray, because of something called hair dye. And my lashes are visible from the moon because of mascara. Repeat after me, mass-care-*ahhh*."

"What's your point?" He percolated with hope.

"Let's take the *ill* out of *Billy* and put some color on those cheeks...the face ones."

She launched herself off the bed and stood with renewed purpose. "I suggest a makeover. Then a takeover. Who's with me?"

Billy considered this. If anything, it would be a fun distraction. And he'd be lying if he said he wasn't curious to see what he looked like after all these years. "You're right. It's time to show Frankie what she's been missing."

"I couldn't agree more," Candace said, slinging a silver handbag over her shoulder. "Let's shop!" She made a move toward her bedroom door and fell flat on her fluffy sheepskin rug. *Oof!*

Billy burst out laughing.

"My laces!" she cackled, discovering the knots.

"I had to," he said. "One last hurrah, for old times' sake."

CHAPTER FIVE
THE HEART SPACE WANTS WHAT THE HEART SPACE WANTS

The forty-five-minute drive to Bridgeport Village had been worth it. Buying a new phone online couldn't possibly have compared to the experience of walking into an Apple Store for the first time. Sleek technology eager to be touched. Built by geniuses. Charged by electricity. Brought to life with the swipe of a fingertip. Frankie considered changing her name to iStein and moving in.

Viveka feigned interest in the laptops with a tight-lipped smile and semi-curious nod. "It's nice to leave Salem every now and then," she said, keeping her daughter close, just in case.

"I agree," Frankie said, indulging her mother, even though she knew Viveka's comment was about more than spending Sunday afternoon phone shopping in Portland. It meant not having to wonder if a shop owner would check their IDs before allowing them into the store. Not mistaking the wind for the sound of someone coming to take them away. Not checking the Internet for slanderous posts. Not dodging suspicious glances from the driver of a passing car. Not questioning their decision to stay and fight what seemed like a losing battle.

"Do you have the gift card?" Viveka asked, her violet eyes void of their usual spark.

Frankie snapped open her quilted black handbag-slash-portable-amp-machine, feeling a sudden sense of superiority over the displayed electronics. Unlike them, she could go for days without a power cord—something they, in their fancy minimalist world, could only dream of.

"Can I browse?" she asked, handing over the envelope from Vlad.

Viveka scanned the perimeter with the side-eyed subtlety of a Secret Service agent. Kids played interactive games at a low circular table, an older couple held a salesman hostage with questions about Macs versus PCs, hipsters grazed, and three bleached blonds in futuristic outfits hovered over the latest iPad. "Fine. But don't wander off. I won't be long."

Normally Frankie would have mocked her mother for being overprotective, but considering the circumstances, she promised to stay close, and then hurried away before she changed her mind.

Intrigued by the blonds' fascination with whatever they were watching, Frankie inched toward them.

The sound was unmistakable. Fearless. Empowered. Revolutionary. *The world premiere of Lady Gaga's new video!* To avoid sparking, she stuffed her hands into the pockets of her skinny military cargoes and asked if she could watch it with them.

They didn't dare turn away from Gaga to respond, but a girl wearing a Bubble Wrap scarf made room. Just as Frankie snagged a decent view, the video ended.

"Best one ever!" declared the blond wearing ice-cream-sprinkle-covered sunglasses on top of her head.

"You say that after every one," said the girl with crime-scene tape tied around her leggings.

"Wait until the concert," said Bubble Wrap.

Frankie gasped. "You're going to her concert?"

"Thirteen more days!" Sprinkle Glasses beamed.

"You?" asked Crime Scene, unaware of the red lipstick smudge on her front tooth.

"I wish." Frankie sighed. "It's impossible to get tickets without a connection."

"Not true," declared Bubble Wrap, putting her arms around Crime Scene and Sprinkle Glasses. "We camped."

Frankie, feeling an instant bond through their mutual love of Gaga, confessed, "I've been a little monster since the day I was born. A few weeks ago, I put white streaks in my hair and..."

Suddenly, Viveka grabbed Frankie by the back of her black-and-pink-striped turtleneck and yanked her out of the store.

"*What?* Mom, what are you doing? Did you get the phones?"

"No talking until we're in the car!" Viveka insisted. "Not a single word."

Something must have happened with the gift card. Something embarrassing.

Viveka slammed the Volvo door, turned up the radio—*in case someone is listening?*—and seethed. "What were you *thinking*?"

"Me?" Frankie sparked. "What did I do?"

Viveka jammed the key into the ignition. "Don't give me that innocent routine. How could you, Frankie? After everything that's happened? *How?*"

Frankie giggled nervously. "Mom, what did I *do*?"

"Telling those strangers you were born a *monster*?" She turned off the ignition and lowered her head into her hands. "It's one thing to put yourself in danger—*again!*—but that term? It's so derogatory. What has happened to you?"

Frankie burst out laughing.

Viveka turned to her in disbelief. Her sleek black ponytail was unusually disheveled. "So this is funny to you?"

"Mom, if I wanted to come out, I'd start by scrubbing off this pore-clogging makeup."

"Then what—"

" 'Little monster' is a Lady Gaga thing. It's what she calls her fans. It has nothing to do with RADs."

"What?"

"Yeah. I was hardly turning myself in."

"Really?"

Frankie raised her brows as if to say, *Come on, Mom, give me some credit.*

A smile, gradual as the rising sun, brightened Viveka's face. The spark in her violet eyes returned. "What a relief." She pulled Frankie in for a gardenia-scented hug and then burst into a mix of laughter and tears.

"I'm sure." Frankie giggled again. "Now, did you get the phones?"

"Got 'em."

Once they were on the highway, Viveka said, "Looks like you're coping with this a lot better than I am." Drops of rain spotted the windshield.

"Not really," Frankie admitted.

Viveka glanced at her daughter with concern.

"I should be thinking of ways to unite everyone, but every time I try, my mind goes back to Brett." Frankie sighed. "I still can't believe he used me like that." Saying it out loud made her chest tighten.

"I can only imagine how painful that is." Viveka rested her hand on Frankie's shoulder.

The truth was, not having Brett in her life anymore hurt more than the betrayal part. But her rational mother would never see the logic in that. *How can you possibly miss someone who caused you pain?* Viveka would ask. Frankie would respond with a *beats me* shrug and would end up feeling more pathetic than she already did.

"Maybe there's a lesson here," Viveka offered, forever the professor.

Frankie gazed out at the *whoosh*ing cars. She didn't want a lesson. She wanted Brett.

"Maybe, you know, until normies become more tolerant, you could get to know some of the RAD boys a little better. Those Wolf brothers are cute."

Mom, you sound just as bad as they do! Frankie wanted to

shout, but she didn't. There was some truth in her mother's advice. Why ask for trouble? It made perfect sense. But perfect sense has nothing to do with feelings.

The heart space wants what the heart space wants.

Unfortunately, Frankie's heart space wanted Brett.

CHAPTER SIX
MAMA TRAUMA

The Jackson crisis was solved. He was staying. With that out of the way, Melody was free to focus on the other issue—the one she had been trying desperately to avoid.

But that was impossible.

Her conversation with Manu at the *Teen Vogue* shoot clung to her brain like a felt skirt over tights.

"Is your mother here?" he asked.

"No, I came with my sister."

"Well." He sighed, like someone recalling a fond memory. *"Tell Marina that Manu says hi. It's been way too long."*

"I think you have me confused with someone else."

"Oh no," he scoffed. *"That voice is unmistakable. Just like your mother's. Marina could get anyone to do absolutely anything; it was that intoxicating."*

"*Sorry, but my mom is Glory. Glory Carver. From California.*"

"*Are you sure?*"

"*Manu, of course she's sure,*" Cleo snapped. "*I think she knows who her mother is.*"

He was staring at Melody's face in a way that would have royally creeped Cleo out if she didn't know him. "*Manu!*"

He shook his head. "*You're right. I am thinking of someone else. I remember hearing that Marina's daughter had a very unforgettable nose. It almost looked like a camel's humps,*" *he chuckled.* "*And yours is perfect. My mistake. I'm sorry.*"

Now old photos of Melody fluttered around her bare feet like leaves in a fall breeze. They settled as the fan rotated left, then fluttered again when it turned right. It was hard to say how long she had been under her sleep loft, mesmerized by flapping pictures and whirring blades. Ten minutes? An hour? All afternoon? It didn't matter. The flaps and whirs provided a steady rhythm. Something she could count on. Something she could trust.

So she had spent Sunday morning foraging through old scrapbooks, searching for a way to discredit Manu's assertion, and then passed the afternoon studying each photo. Did her presurgery nose *really* look like camel humps? Maybe she resembled her mother more as a toddler than she did now. Or perhaps there was at least one picture of her in the hospital, wrapped in a pink blanket, nuzzled against Glory's chest. Because there were, like, thirty thousand photos of baby Candace.

After a thorough analysis, there was no evidence to support

Manu's claim, yet none to the contrary, either. The only real conclusion was that if Melody wanted answers, she'd have to ask questions. And so she sat, in her striped J.Crew pajamas, teeth unbrushed, hair smelling like doughnuts from her visit to Crystal's Coffee, debating the benefit of knowing the truth.

Of course, if Glory said, "I am without a doubt your real mother," and offered indisputable proof, everything would be perfect. But any other response would mean one more place she didn't belong.

"Candace!" Glory called, padding down the hallway. "Please tell me you have my white silk tunic and it's *clean*."

Melody rolled her eyes, grateful for the lock on her door. *Must be nice when a missing tunic is your biggest problem.*

"I thought Dad was packing for you," Melody heard Candace say. "Isn't that part of your anniversary tradition thingy?"

"Technically, yes, but last year he packed a tablecloth instead of a sarong, and I'm not taking another chance. I'm bringing an extra purse full of essentials." She lowered her voice. "Let's keep this between us, shall we?"

More secrets. Typical.

"I dunno," Candace stalled. She had obviously lost the tunic, stained it, or sold it. "Dad's surprising you with this whole vacation, and part of it is packing for you. I think it's romantic. You should just go with it, Mom. Forget the tunic. Surrender."

"Candace, this is not the time for games," her mother insisted. "He'll be home any minute and—"

"Glo-reee," called Beau, opening the front door. "Glo-reee!"

"Find it," she hissed, before calling out, "I'm up here."

His boots scuffed along the worn wooden steps as he climbed

upstairs. "You're not going to believe it," he said with a sigh. "The Hideout Inn is closed for some private function!"

"What? Are you sure?" Glory gasped. "The Kramers will be here in less than an hour. What am I supposed to serve?"

Melody's insides dipped. She'd totally forgotten that the plastic surgeon and his family were coming for dinner.

"I tried Aegean Blue and Russo's, but they were boarded up. So I got Mandarin Palace."

"Ew," Candace grumbled.

"I bet it has to do with that TV show," Glory stated.

"What? You think the restaurants were owned by RADs?" Beau asked. The word sounded awkward coming from him. Like when he said "awesome" or "text me."

"I wouldn't be surprised," Glory said. "Maybe they left town."

"Aren't you being a little dramatic?" Beau asked.

A prickly rush of anxiety passed through Melody. Jackson had come so close to leaving. *What if I hadn't been able to stop him?*

"A few of the gals at the salon got to talking today, and some elderly woman getting a perm said RADs should be forced to live on a barge in the middle of the Pacific. She's still haunted by the movie *Frankenstein*, and she said to this day people with square-shaped heads give her panic attacks. The poor thing can't even look at Arnold Schwarzenegger without collapsing. Her words."

"Biddy out," Candace said.

Melody couldn't help giggling. Even in the darkest times, her sister could always lighten the mood.

"Personally, I don't see what the big deal is," Glory added. "As long as these RADs don't affect my life, I don't care what they do—unless they clip their fingernails in public. I can't stand when *anyone* does that. It's vile. Okay, I'd better get that food into some Pyrex before my cover is blown. Candace, tell Melly it's time to stop studying. Dinner is in a half hour. She needs to shower."

"Did ya hear that?" Candace asked, knocking on Melody's door. "Mom thinks you're dirty." Melody reluctantly got up and unlocked the door.

"It smells like depression in here," Candace said, barging in. "What's up?" Her hair was in a high ponytail; her snowy eye shadow and frosty gloss were Sunday casual. "Jackson didn't change his mind and bail, did he?"

Melody shook her head.

"Did your hairbrush?"

Melody stood there, ignoring the jab. Her knees were sore, and her butt was tingling. How long had she been sitting on the floor, anyway? "Can I ask you something?"

Candace looked down at her chest. "Yes, they're real."

"Come on, this is important." The words, sticky with emotion, barely made it past Melody's throat.

Candace leaned against the far wall and folded her arms across her ivory slip dress. "Ask away."

Swallowing her trepidation, Melody blurted, "Remember I asked you if you had ever heard of someone named Marina?"

Candace nodded a little too hard. She loved making her ponytail swing.

"Well, I asked because when we were at the *Teen Vogue* shoot and I sang to those camels, Manu told me I sounded exactly like

68

my mother, *Marina*. When I told him Mom's name was Glory, he looked like he didn't believe me. Until he remembered that Marina's daughter had a nose that looked like camel humps." Melody grabbed a handful of photos off the floor and held them out in front of her. "And look...*humps*!"

"So ask Mom," Candace suggested, as if they were talking about a second serving of pie.

"I can't."

"Why?"

Melody shrugged. How could she explain to her fearless sister that she was afraid of the truth? That she'd rather live in uncertainty than know she wasn't part of the family? That—

"Maaaah-mmmm," Candace called.

"What are you *doing*?"

Candace called again.

"Stop! Candace, please—"

"What?" Glory called from the kitchen.

"Can you come up here for a sec? Melly has something important to ask you and Dad!"

Melody's jaw hung slack. Shock gripped her speeding heart and squeezed. She wanted to pummel her sister. Beat her into a frothy mousse. Jam her hair in the fan and watch it tangle.

"Is everything okay?" Glory asked, pushing the door open. She was wearing YSL oven mitts (a gift from an A-list chef she had styled back in Beverly Hills).

"What's up?" Beau asked, peeking in behind her. "Why aren't you dressed, Melly? The Kramers will be here any minute."

"Ask them," Candace urged. And then she left.

Her parents' expression was a mix of concern and impatience.

"Um." Melody inhaled deeply. *When I can't hold my breath any longer, I'll ask.*

Her chest began to tighten.

Her head started to throb.

She became light-headed.

Her body was aching.

"What is it, Melly?" Glory asked, stepping forward. "Cramps?"

"Does she need a muscle relaxer?" Beau asked his wife, obviously too squeamish to talk menstruation with his daughter. "I have some—"

Whoooooooooooooooooooooosh. Melody exhaled. "Who's Marina?"

"*Who?*" Glory asked.

"Marina? Do you know a woman named Marina?" Melody spoke more slowly.

"No." Glory shook her head.

"Someone from a long time ago, maybe?"

"Never heard of her. Why?"

"What's this about?" Beau interjected.

Relief coated Melody's insides. Her shoulders relaxed back into their sockets. Her heart slowed. *Manu was wrong!*

Having the answer to the million-dollar question, she could have highlight-deleted the topic and moved on. After all, there was plenty of Jackson drama to focus on. But the billion-dollar question had yet to be answered, and according to the movie *The Social Network*, billion was the new million. So it needed to be asked.

Melody took another deep breath and waited for the pain to force it out of her.

"Momareyoumybirthmother?" she blurted.

Glory gasped and then covered her mouth. Her blue-green eyes widened, and she glanced sideways at Beau. He put his hand on her YSL oven mitt, reminding her he was there.

Oh. My. GOD!

Blood thumped against the insides of Melody's ears. Her gums. Her scalp. She was going to throw up. Every object in the room seemed floaty; every sound, hollow. Over time, the moment would sharpen. It would inhabit her mind with HD clarity as the moment that changed her life forever.

"Are you kidding me?" Melody shouted.

"We can explain," Glory began. "As soon as dinner is over, we'll sit down and—"

"I'm not hungry!"

Melody needed air. Sliding on a pair of flip-flops and reaching for the nearest hoodie, she pushed past her parents and hurried down the steps.

"Where are you going?" Beau called. "The Kramers will be here in ten minutes. They want to meet the family."

"Then I guess you won't be needing me!" Melody yelled, slamming the front door shut behind her.

CHAPTER SEVEN
SPLIT, SHOWER, AND SHAVE

This Wolf was getting hoarse.

If I leave one more message, I'll be talking like Demi, Clawdeen thought as she tossed the Motorola Karma onto her bed. *Where is everyone? Why am I getting sent to voice mail? And why isn't anyone calling me back?* If it hadn't been for the tower of Sassy RSVPs on her desk — twenty-seven yeses and zero nos — she'd be doubting her fabulousness in a major way.

Anxious to visit her friends and get some answers, Clawdeen peeked through her bedroom window for what felt like the trillionth time. It wouldn't be long now....

The normie gawkers were finally packing up their cameras and heading home. A dead-end street inhabited mostly by "monsters" was obviously not where they wanted to be now that the sun was setting. Which suited Clawdeen just fine. She had been hiding out in her bedroom all day, subjected to the clang and clatter of Clawd's free weights on the other side of the wall. Forbidden to poke her nose outside and sniff the crisp fall air. Banned from playing music, turning on lights, or walking near windows—anything that might alert people that they were back. If only she had been allowed to go online. She'd have updated her Facebook status to *Rapunzel*.

Confinement, however, hadn't been a *total* waste. After sleeping until noon, Clawdeen spent fifty minutes in a fur-free shower with her fruit-scented products and a fresh Gillette Venus. She jammed her oversized Hideout Inn gift shop clothes in the back of Don's closet and slid on a black ruffled V-neck and the Hudsons that gave her booty melon-scoop roundness. She painted earth-toned rainbows on her nails and packed a roller bag of toiletries and clothing essentials to take back to the inn.

Clawdeen dialed Lala, Blue, Frankie, Julia, Billy, Jackson, and even Deuce. Still, she got nothing but voice mails. *Fur real?*

Suddenly, a thought more alarming than ADT rang through her mind. *What if they'd been forced to leave too?* The silky auburn hair on the back of her neck shot up. They couldn't! Her party was two weeks away. There were playlists to discuss, centerpieces to build, dresses to alter, makeup to test, hairstyles to try, kiss wish-lists to craft, and Cleo's un-vitation to draft.

Hhh-ugh!

Her headboard—a chain-link fence she'd spray-painted gold—rattled as Clawd grunt-dropped his weights.

"Enough, already!" she shouted, banging on the wall. "It's dark out. The normies are gone. Let's gooooooo!"

The sticky rip of Velcro separating meant he was taking off his gloves. *Awoooo!* Five minutes in the shower, and big bro was finally ready. Clawdeen slipped on her crimson suede flats and grabbed her suitcase, video camera, sewing kit, glue gun, glitter paints, and the Sassy dress she'd been working on, in case they had to make another run for it. Preparing for the worst wasn't something she'd ordinarily do, but two days in gift shop garb will do that to a girl.

"Let me go first," Clawd said, holding back his sister with a freshly pumped-up forearm. Sandalwood-scented aftershave, along with strands of brown hair, clung to his blazer. He reached for the brass doorknob with the shaky apprehension of a horror-film actor.

Clawdeen giggled. "A little dramatic, don'tcha think?"

"Says the girl with the luggage."

Clawdeen pushed past him and opened the door herself. The night breeze, a cool kiss on the cheek, was refreshing compared to the stale air of an abandoned house.

Something about the neighborhood was different—borderline eerie. Avoiding the streetlamps, they trespassed from one neighbor's lawn to the next. Peering inside windows and rapping lightly on panes with their fingernails.

Signs of life were everywhere: recycle bins left curbside, kitchen lights on, dinner tables set, food in serving dishes. TVs tuned to Channel Two, muddy sneakers by front doors, bicycles in driveways.…The only things missing were the lives themselves.

"Where *is* everyone?" Clawdeen asked, tapping the mermaid knocker on Blue's side door. The dolphin fountains in the yard were still spurting water, and the jets in the black-bottomed pools were whipping up frothy bubbles. "It's like everyone... vanished."

"Have you tried calling?"

Clawdeen shot him a *did-you-honestly-just-ask-me-such-a-stupid-question?* glare.

The bloodred leaves of a Japanese maple rustled overhead. Clawd lifted a finger to his lips and held his sister by the sleeve.

"Relax," Clawdeen muttered, heart thumping. "It's just the wind."

"No," he insisted, cocking his ear toward the street. "I hear footsteps."

Clawdeen knew better than to argue with her brother about his keen sense of hearing. It was even better than hers. She peered past his shoulder.

"It's a girl. She's running... wearing sneakers... sniffling... sick... no, not sick... crying. Stand back!" He forced her against the cold glass exterior of Aunt Coral's house.

Just then Melody Carver ran past the yard. Clawdeen's chest inflated with joy.

"Mel—" she began to yelp. Clawd covered her mouth.

"Are you *crazy*?"

Clawdeen licked his salty palm until he removed it. "Why do you think she was crying? Maybe she knows something. We should find her and..."

"She's a normie. We can't trust her. Besides, what's *she* gonna know?"

Clawdeen considered reminding him that Melody was dating Jackson. That she was on their side. And that being a normie didn't automatically make someone an enemy. She had twenty-seven yes RSVPs to prove it. But Clawd seemed too rattled to listen to reason. Funny, since their father had put him in charge. "Well, we can't give up yet."

"Fine. One more house. How about..." He paused as if contemplating and then casually suggested Lala's.

Zigzagging up the block, they walked in what felt like an endless W. Up the side of one house, down the next, up one, down the next, with Clawdeen dragging her suitcase over uncut grass.

Finally, the old Victorian was next. Hidden under a canopy of branches and maple leaves, Lala's house was the best concealed on the block. The inside was always dark, but the flicker from Uncle Vlad's candelabra usually filled it with life. Tonight there were no flickers. There was no sign of life.

Car lights shone at the top of the block. "Follow me," Clawd hissed, disappearing under the trees.

Clawdeen tried, but the wheels of her suitcase kept jamming. She yanked. "I'm trying."

The lights were getting closer. Clawd doubled back, lifted the suitcase with one hand, and dragged his sister behind a maple tree with the other. Seconds later, a BMW sedan with the license plate KRAMER 1 rolled by slowly, as if searching for something... or someone.

"We have to get out of here," Clawd insisted.

"What about Lala?"

"She's obviously not home," he said, tilting his head toward the still house.

"Let's try the underground. Maybe they're hiding there."

"Might as well." Clawd smacked a falling leaf. "It's not like we can go home now."

The eight-block drive to the Riverfront was postapocalyptic. Salem was lifeless, ghostly.

"I'm glad we're here," Clawdeen said, glancing at Clawd's profile as he gripped the wheel. His facial features were perfectly proportioned. His eyes weren't spread out like Rocks's. His nose wasn't as wide as Howie's. And his lips were full, but not puffy like Nino's. Even Clawd's cheekbones were the perfect height. Compared to Don's, they were like bunk beds next to a California king.

"Admit it, you're glad I came."

"That depends," he said, refusing to take his eyes off the barren road ahead.

"On what?"

"On whether I get you home safely."

"Clawd, I'm only a year younger than you. You can stop worrying about me," she insisted. But she knew his concern went deeper than that. Worrying about women was instinctive for the Wolfs. The males were stronger. Their hearing was better. They ran faster. Those were the facts. Still, bravery and brains counted for something, and Clawdeen had come fully loaded with those.

Once inside the RADs' headquarters at RIP, the siblings stood and stared at the stone pile of credit cards and cell phones.

"That would explain the unanswered phone calls," Clawdeen mumbled.

Clawd was too stunned to respond. They walked back to the car in silence.

Had her friends really left town? An entire community wiped out by a TV show? Where was their courage? Their pride? Their etiquette? Didn't they know it was rude to bail on a function after RSVP'ing yes?

"My Sassy is so not happening," Clawdeen sobbed on the drive home.

Clawd looked at her incredulously. "*That*'s what you're worried about? Your *party*?"

"No." She sniffled. It wasn't *all* she was worried about, but it was up there. For once something was going to be all about her. Not her brothers, her friends, the family business, or the RADs. Just her. Clawdeen Lucia Wolf. Not that she'd ever admit it to someone who was happy with a twelve-pack of sweat socks and a box of powdered doughnuts for his birthday. "I'm just saying, we have to find everyone. We have to bring them back and make things normal again."

"If by *we* you mean two *other* people, then I agree. Because *you*'re heading back tonight. Our instincts to hide were right. It's obviously not safe, or everyone would still be here."

"What about you?"

"Coach said I could stay with him tonight." Out of habit, Clawd turned onto Radcliffe Way. He quickly reversed and headed for their new spot three blocks over. "I'm picking up my uniform, then I'm taking you back to the inn."

"Well, if you're staying, I'm staying."

"Over my hairy body," Clawd said, turning off the car. "I'm not taking responsibility for you anymore. It's too much pressure. I have to focus on football and..."

In an act of desperation, Clawdeen pulled the keys out of the ignition, jumped out of the car, and chucked them into the ravine.

"Looks like we're both staying now."

Clawd hurried to the edge of the brush but knew it was too dark. Exasperated, he grabbed fistfuls of his own hair and pulled. "Are you *insane*?"

Thrumming with adrenaline, Clawdeen began making her way back home. *Insane* was probably the right word, but she preferred *determined*.

CHAPTER EIGHT
HOOKY MONSTER

Frankie and Cleo stood frozen in disbelief at the head of the concrete path that led to the mustard-yellow building. The lawn was abuzz with demonstrations. If a March on Washington were to take place on Halloween, it would look like Merston High that Monday morning.

To the left, a smattering of RAD supporters wore monster costumes and chanted, *"Don't hate, tol-er-ate! It's un-NUDI to discriminate!"* Frankie recognized Melody's sister, Candace, instantly. She had cut holes in a rhinestone-studded sleep mask and wore a normie-flesh-toned bodysuit with the word NUDI written in fuchsia lipstick where bikini tops usually go. Two of her friends were raising a skull-and-crossbones flag up the flagpole.

"What do pirates have to do with this?" Cleo asked.

"Ayyyye dunno," Frankie tried in her best pirate voice. "But it's pretty voltage! They're taking our side. I wish Blue, Lala, and Clawdeen were around to see this."

"Yeah, all five of them are taking our side. Golden," Cleo hissed, and then began making her way up the path, purposely trying to stay a few steps ahead of Frankie.

But what did Frankie expect? They'd only walked to school together because no one else was around. All they had in common was a fear of being exposed.

Frankie was the new girl. A product of modern technology; a hint of things to come. Cleo, on the other hand, was ancient royalty. Her handbag held priceless gems. Frankie's? Batteries. The amber-scented princess was wearing gold wedges, army-green jeggings, a long camel-colored tank, an ivory faux-fur vest, and sleeves of jingling, mismatched bangles. Her outfit was red carpet, while Frankie's turtleneck dress was more like wall-to-wall. But she didn't have the luxury of obsessing over the superficial. Not today.

To their right, a group of sixty-plus parents and students, led by normie Bekka Madden, chanted, *"Keep us all safe from harm, send the monsters to a farm!"* The wack-tivist even tried comedy: *"Did you hear about the Steins' hockey game? There was a face-off in the corner!"* Her followers cheered her on, jabbing MONSTER HIGH signs through the thinning morning fog, looking pleased with themselves. As if their wannabe-clever trick—rearranging the letters in their school's name—was Pulitzer-worthy. Frankie couldn't help wondering what side of the lawn Brett would choose. Today was the day she'd find out. She managed to slip her fingers inside the sleeves of her dress right before they sparked.

81

"Is that normie fur real?" Cleo asked, borrowing Clawdeen's favorite expression.

The scene reminded Frankie of her first high school experience. Ignoring her parents' advice, she had arrived makeup-free and scared the pom-poms off a group of cheerleaders. Thankfully, it was a Sunday, the school was in another town, and she had escaped unharmed. Sort of. Mentally, Frankie was scarred; her pride was wounded, confidence shot. Why did people like Bekka Madden get to decide what was acceptable and what wasn't?

"You're not going to believe it," said Billy, suddenly joining them.

"Ahhh!" yelped Frankie, startled.

"Daryl Komen and Eli Shaw are giving people monster tests by the sophomore lockers."

"Go onnnn," muttered Cleo, like a spy.

"Yeah, what's a monster test?" Frankie asked, directing the question at Cleo instead of the Starburst-scented air, in case anyone was watching. She knew they were safe for now—their identities hadn't been revealed on TV—but this was hardly the day to get caught with an invisible friend.

"They're checking mouths for fangs, pulling off sunglasses… that kind of thing."

"Thank Geb I wasn't in that film," Cleo said, twirling a chunky blond highlight around her self-righteous fingers.

"Speaking of which," Billy said, gripping the top of Frankie's head and angling it toward the parking lot. Heath Burns was getting out of his sister's blue Prius. Brett, who always rode with them, was not. "Look who decided to skip school today. Told you he was guilty."

Frankie's heart space clenched. *Did Billy have to sound so amped about it?*

"Heath!" she called, taking off without saying good-bye.

He turned. "Oh, hey." He smiled, relieved. His eyes darted across the lawn. "Y-you okay?" he asked quietly.

"Fine, you?"

He nodded, then thumb-flicked a white Tums into his mouth, obviously trying to keep his fire-burps under control.

"Is this freaky or what?" he asked, jerking a thumb at the demonstrators. "Guess I'm lucky I was working the camera, or I would have been exposed too."

"Where's Brett?"

Heath pulled her toward the Prius, refusing to answer until he was out of earshot.

"Have you seen him?" Frankie tried again.

He bit into another chalky tablet and then shook his head. "Not since..."

"Do you think he set us up?"

Rolling his eyes, he said, "My sister does. She never liked him. But I don't think so."

"Have you tried calling him?"

"Voice mail every time. You?"

"I don't have his contact info. It was in my old phone, and..." Frankie stopped herself, wondering if the excuse sounded as silly to him as it had to her. After all, she was made of synthetic body parts. Fueled by electricity. Kept alive by a rockin' handbag. If technology was capable of all that, shouldn't she be able to track down a cell?

Heath thumbed through his mobile and then sighed. "I hope he's okay."

Okay?

Never once had Frankie considered the possibility that Brett might be in danger. Not that she wanted him to be hurt. But if he was, that would mean he hadn't betrayed her. He and Bekka would not be in cahoots with Hollywood. Her mother would be wrong about "sticking to her own kind." And she would be free to crush on him again, to save him the way he'd saved her. A dam burst inside Frankie. Hope surged toward her heart space.

Heath rattled off Brett's number just as the first bell rang. Protesters tucked their signs under their arms and began racing up the steps.

"Let me know if you hear anything," said the pin-thin redhead, flipping up his green hood and hurrying toward the entrance.

Frankie stayed by the Prius. Once her fingers stopped sparking, she began composing her text.

U OK?

(Delete.) She sounded too concerned. What if Brett had betrayed her?

HEATH IS WORRIED ABOUT U. PLS CALL.

(Delete.) He might call Heath and not her.

I DESERVE AN EXPLANATION, DON'TCHA THINK?

(Delete.) Too angry. What if he's in trouble?

84

KNOCK ONCE FOR DANGER. TWICE FOR BETRAYAL.
(Delete.) Too glib.
LOVE TO HEAR UR SIDE OF THE STORY.

The final bell rang. Frankie's thumb hovered over the SEND button. Was this the one? She read it one last time. The tone seemed free of judgment, curious in case he was innocent, yet firm in case he wasn't.

She hit SEND and waited…and waited…and waited….

Checking her phone every forty-five seconds didn't pay off until the end of third period, when Brett finally wrote back. Starving, Frankie devoured the white conversation bubble in a single glance.

BRETT: CAN'T HELP U. DON'T CONTACT ME AGAIN.

Limp with disappointment, Frankie couldn't bring herself to respond. There was nothing more to say. His bubble was clear. Hers had burst.

CHAPTER NINE
LOOTY CALL

Vroooom. Vrooom.

Melody woke to the sound of a revving motorcycle. Eyes sting-ing, insides weighted with sorrow. Something distressing had happened the night before. Her body remembered, but her mind was too hazy to recall the details.

Vroooom. Vrooom. That grating noise had to go. She buried her head under her pillow. And then, in a flash of clarity, she rec-ognized her own ringtone. *Please be Jackson.* She fumbled around her lavender sheets and found her iPhone. "Hullo?"

"Where are you?"

Melody flopped back down and closed her eyes. "Hey, Can-dace." She peered outside to gauge the hour. The view was dark-ened by the caramel-colored tint on the pane. "What time is it?"

"One thirty. Peee-em! Haven't you been reading your texts?"

TO: Melly
oct 18, 7:06 AM
CANDACE: BEKKA PROTESTING AT SCHOOL!!! NUDIS MUST REPRESENT. HURRY!

TO: Melly
oct 18, 7:19 AM
CANDACE: BILLY SNEAKED INTO ART STUDIO. MAKING SIGNS NOW. GET OVER HERE.

TO: Melly
oct 18, 7:34 AM
CANDACE: BILLY SNEAKED INTO DRAMA ROOM TO GET MASKS FOR PROTEST. GIMMICKS GET MEDIA ATTENTION.

TO: Melly
oct 18, 8:10 AM
CANDACE: HUNG A FLAG! FOUND IT IN A BIN MARKED "PIRATES OF PENZANCE PROPS." BUT IT TOTALLY WORKS! U HERE YET?

TO: Melly
oct 18, 9:07 AM
CANDACE: PRINCIPAL WEEKS SAYS HE'S NOT TAKING SIDES. BUT IN THE NAME OF FREEDOM OF SPEECH— OR EXPRESSION (I FORGET)—WE CAN PROTEST. WHERE R U???? IF YOU'RE STILL AT HOME BRING MY SOUND FX CD.

TO: Melly
oct 18, 12:22 PM
CANDACE: DIDN'T SEE JACKSON, CLAWDEEN, LALA, BLUE, DEUCE, OR THE HOT WOLF BROTHERS DURING LUNCH. R THEY OKAY? ALSO, DIDN'T SEE BILLY. HA!

TO: Melly
oct 18, 1:10 PM
CANDACE: BEKKA IS SELLING TICKETS FOR SOME MYSTERIOUS AFTER-SCHOOL THING. BILLY IS SPYING TO GET INFO. MIGHT BE A FUND-RAISER. SOMETHING TO CONSIDER FOR NUDI. WE NEED $ FOR COSTUMES AND A SLOGAN WRITER.

TO: Melly
oct 18, 1:24 PM
CANDACE: TIRED OF TEXTING. I'M CALLING YOU. PICK UP!

"Melly," Candace continued. "Do I need to have you examined? I'll call a doctor if you want. Just don't die while Mom and Dad are away. They'll never leave me in charge again."

"I'm fine," Melody grumbled. A bird feather—dusty blue and olive, with a golden tip—landed on her thigh. She was still wearing the striped J.Crew pajamas. The ones she wore last night...when she ran out on dinner....Suddenly, the details came rushing back.

The knowing glance her parents had exchanged when she asked if Glory was her birth mother...the probability that she was adopted...skipping out on the Kramers...seeing Clawdeen and her brother getting into a car...hiding in the bushes because she didn't want them to see her cry (which must explain the bird feather)...waiting outside until the Kramers left...stomping past her parents and heading straight for bed...insisting they leave, even though they offered to cancel their trip...pretending to be asleep when they kissed her good-bye at four thirty AM before heading to the airport...ignoring Candace when she came in to wake her up for school....

The fifth-period bell *bwoop*ed in the background. "Gotta go," Candace said into the phone. "Oh, by the way, you owe me big for leaving me with those *Kramers*. Either they didn't think the 'Mia Rosen's face-plant off the high dive' was a funny story, or they rode the Botox bus to Cannotsmile Station. I swear, it was like eating at Madame Tussauds." The bell *bwoop*ed again. "Candace out."

After a much-needed shower, Melody contemplated her next move over a bowl of Cap'n Crunch's Crunch Berries.

What would Jackson do? (*Crunch, crunch, crunch.*) What would Jackson do? (*Crunch, crunch, crunch.*) What would

Jackson do? (*Crunch, crunch, crunch.*) A valid question, since Ms. J had kept the truth from him too, simply never bothering to mention that he was a RAD who was sharing a body with D.J. Hyde. Yet he had handled the situation with bravery and grace. He'd sought the answers, accepted them, and then adapted. *Seek, accept, adapt*…three principles Melody had resisted her entire life. Typically, she sat back and hoped things would change because they were unjust. Bullies, liars, snobs…the universe would even the score eventually. When it didn't, she would become cynical and angry. Then withdrawn. Never once had she considered changing things herself. Until now.

Until Jackson.

Light-headed from her day of sleeping—or was it her night of crying?—Melody stepped out onto the sun-soaked street in search of answers. She had traded her striped pajamas for a fitted military jacket (*thanks, Candace!*), faded thrift-shop Wranglers, pink Converse, and a look of determination. Her black hair was in a sleek *let's-get-down-to-business* ponytail, and her narrow gray eyes were dry. She could practically hear Jackson cheering her on.

Regal and stoic, 32 Radcliffe Way seemed more intimidating than usual. It had taken on the appearance of a sprawling, three-story vault. Dutifully guarding the person who held the secrets of her past. Finger trembling, Melody pressed the doorbell and took a step back. Soft bells chimed on the other side. A security camera lens was the first to greet her. The bald, dark-skinned man she had come to see was second. Lips pursed, he smiled. Had he been expecting her?

"Melody, right?" he asked, with a mild Middle Eastern accent.

She nodded.

"Cleo's at school." He paused. "That *is* why you're here, isn't it?"

"Actually, I'm here to see you." She stepped inside the dimly lit anteroom. A second door, the one that opened into the house, was shut. Upholstered benches offered a respite for those not welcomed inside.

"Have a seat," he said, gesturing to a bench. He smoothed the front of his white tunic, sat across from her, and waited for her to speak.

"So, um, I've been thinking about what you said, you know, at the photo shoot last week...." Melody's mouth dried. "You know, about Marina."

"Ah, yes." He smacked his thigh playfully. "Marina. The woman who is *not* your mother."

"Well, that's just it. It turns out she might be—"

The front door clicked open. Amber-scented perfume seeped in. Cleo followed.

"*Melody?*" She dropped her gold metallic tote on the reed carpet. Her ivory faux-fur vest and jingling bangles were proof that she was not lying low like the other RADs. "Hey, why weren't you at school today?" asked the princess, tossing her black-and-gold-streaked hair.

"I wasn't feeling so great."

"Maybe some fresh air will do you both good," Manu suggested.

Cleo rolled her kohl-lined eyes, kissed his bald head, and giggled. "I swear, you sound like Father."

Manu stood and placed his arm around Cleo's shoulder and

91

gave her a loving squeeze. "I *have* helped raise you since you were born," he said. And then to Melody: "You know, a person doesn't have to be biologically linked to a child to be a parent. At the same time, biological parents aren't always the best ones to raise us. Families come in many forms. What's important is that we feel loved and—"

"All right, all right, wrap it up," Cleo joked, like someone who had heard this many times before.

"But wait," Melody said urgently. "What if that person who is being raised by nonbiological parents wants to know more? You know, about her real past and why she...or he was being lied to?"

"No one is lying to me," Cleo said, her eyebrows knit in confusion.

"Then that *person* should find the courage to speak to her parents," Manu said.

"But—"

"For the love of Geb, there's nothing to speak about! My dad travels. I love staying with Manu. It's all golden. Now can we *please* talk about something that matters? My best friends are gone, and Deuce has been in Greece for"—Cleo checked her phone—"eleven hours and hasn't called yet."

"You're right," Manu said, turning the scarab knob on the inner door and stepping into the grand foyer. "I'll leave you girls to more important matters."

"Manu, wait," Melody started, unsatisfied with his clichéd speech about family. But the door closed behind him, and he was gone.

Cleo smoothed the ivory faux fur on her vest and pouted. "What's the point of cute outfits if no one is around to admire them?"

Melody sighed disappointedly.

"Don't worry," Cleo assured her. "I was just being rhetorical. I'll still wear them."

All of a sudden, a familiar female voice blasted through the neighborhood. "HERE WE HAVE THE HOUSE WHERE DRACULA'S SPAWN RESIDES...."

Melody and Cleo bolted outside.

Bekka Madden was standing on Lala's mossy front lawn, clutching a bullhorn and posing with six girls while her sidekick, Haylee, took their picture. Bekka's brown bob had been wrestled into stumpy pigtails, and her usual farm-girl chic had been replaced with a pair of sensible black slacks and a white blouse. She looked like a nun on casual Friday.

"Help yourself to a souvenir from the property," she offered. "For an extra five dollars, Haylee will photograph your treasure in front of the house to prove authenticity—which you'll need if you want to sell it on eBay."

The girls scoured the grounds for the perfect keepsake.

"This is total *ka*!" Cleo hissed.

Melody had no idea what *ka* meant, but she was just as vexed.

"You're trespassing!" Cleo called, stomping across the street. "Get off Lala's property or I'm calling the police."

The girls froze and looked to their tour guide for further instruction.

"Look who it is." Bekka tapped her nails on the bullhorn. "Ignore her," she called to the six girls. "Taking pictures is not a crime."

Cleo placed her hand on her hip. "Well, murder is, and I'm going to kill you if you don't get out of here."

"I have a permit," Bekka announced. She snapped her fingers at Haylee. "Show them."

"Show them what?"

"The *permit*," Bekka insisted. "I put it in there when we left the courthouse. *Re-mem-ber?*" She gritted her teeth.

"Oh yeah," Haylee said, adjusting her beige cat-eye glasses. The mousy sidekick began rifling through her crocodile attaché case. Meanwhile, behind them, the girls were hard at work. One tucked Lala's black doormat under her arm while another began unscrewing the house numbers with a metal nail file. She yanked the 3 loose and quickly went to work on the 7.

Melody spoke up. "Bekka, what you're doing is cruel. Even for you."

"No *way*!" Bekka knocked her forehead. "I can't believe it took me so long to figure this out."

"Figure what out?" Cleo asked, backing away nervously.

"Just when you think you've seen it all…" Bekka called, splaying her arm like a ringmaster. "I give you two actual monsters!"

Cleo gasped. Once again, the girls froze.

Fury and vitriol churned inside Melody. "What are you *talking* about, Bekka?" she yelled. And then to the girls, "Do you actually believe her?"

"Of course they believe me," Bekka shouted through the bullhorn. "Why shouldn't they? You both live on this street. You date known monsters. Ergo, either you *are* monsters or you know where they're hiding."

Cleo, tooth-scraping the gloss off her quivering bottom lip, took a step closer to Melody. Bekka had no shortage of unappealing qualities, but stupidity wasn't one of them.

"These people you're exploiting are harmless," Melody said, more to Haylee and the girls than to Bekka. "They went on TV to show you that they're not going to hurt anyone, and this is how you respond?" An image of Jackson hiding out in some damp, dark basement—alone, without cell service, without *her*—made her insides lurch. "GET OUT OF HERE!" she yelled.

Birds launched off Lala's maple and flapped away. Oddly enough, Bekka, Haylee, and their six-pack followed, scampering up the street like frightened deer.

"How did you *do* that?" Cleo asked.

"I have no idea," Melody admitted as a feather—shimmering muted blues and greens, with a golden tip—drifted onto her shoulder. Absentmindedly, she brushed it to the ground.

"What are you doing?" Cleo asked, picking it up and holding it to the sunlight. "This thing is awesome."

"Yeah," Melody mumbled, her thoughts drifting back to the power of her voice and Manu.

"What bird is *this* from?"

Melody shrugged.

Cleo held it against her collarbone. "How royal would this look as a necklace?"

As a second feather landed on Melody's arm, Cleo quickly snatched it up. She lifted the pair to her head. "Or earrings?"

Melody nodded.

"Can I have them?" Cleo asked, walking backward as she crossed the street to her house.

Melody stayed put. She wanted to be alone. Needed to process. Needed more clarity. "Go for it."

"MONSTERS!" Bekka shouted one last time from the top of the block. "Just wait! I'm gonna prove it!"

"Let me know when you do!" Melody yelled back, meaning it. Maybe then she'd have some answers.

CHAPTER TEN
LORD OF THE FLEAS

While normie kids were enjoying after-school snacks and updating their Facebook pages to the smell of dinner cooking, Clawdeen was on all fours, searching the ravine for the Jetta keys. Keys *she* had tossed the night before because she didn't want Clawd to take her back to the inn. Which, after five hours in a twiggy, leafy, ant-infested, deer poo–peppered gully, no longer seemed like such a bad idea. Compared to this, the inn had been upgraded to spa status. Hopefully, Clawd would return from his football game with good news. If not, the whole *we-have-to-run-back-to-the-inn-and-then-return-with-the-spare-keys* news might not sit so well.

Focus, Clawdeen thought, blinking away her negativity. *Clear your mind and become one with the keys. Focus. Look. Feel....* A mosquito pierced the back of her ear. (*Smack!*) The bugs were loving her new black-currant body wash. The latest buy for her Sassy Sixteen, the signature scent would help ring in a new year and maybe attract a guy...or ten. But who knew if her party would even happen now? Her parents seemed to think it was over, but she refused to—

"We'll head back tomorrow, free of charge," said a girl in the distance. Clawdeen's supersensitive ears perked up. "Bring bikinis. We'll hit up Blue's house and go for a swim."

Blue's house? Who is going to Blue's house? Is she back?

After a round of *yays*, *thank you*s, and smoochy sounds, the group—which sounded no larger than eight—separated. Most continued up the street while two, wearing some seriously unattractive-sounding footwear, rounded the corner toward Clawdeen. She crouched behind a tree and peered up at the sidewalk. Still, they were too far away for her to identify.

"Mark the time and day," insisted the girl speedily, her voice getting louder, closer. "I'm officially going on the record saying those two are hiding something. Something big."

Clawdeen finally got a visual. It was Bekka Madden, dictating her thoughts to her curiously devoted friend Haylee.

"And I'm going to expose it," Bekka said. "They think they scared us just now, but it's them that should be scared."

"Who," Haylee said.

"Cleo and Melody," Bekka snapped.

Cleo is here? Clawdeen wondered.

"No, I mean it's them *who* should be scared. Not them *that* should be scared."

Clawdeen began to growl under her breath. No one threatened her sort-of friend and ex-friend and got away with it—especially not that vengeful normie.

"I bet they're still standing in the middle of their street laughing. But we'll have the last laugh when..."

Standing in the middle of their street? Omigod! Clawdeen fought every urge to jump from the ravine, scratch Bekka's white blouse to ribbons, and charge into the street. She had to warn her friends. Had to stop Bekka. Had to find the keys. Had to...

"Look," said Haylee, pointing at the tree. Clawdeen held her breath, sucked in her stomach, and squeezed her eyes shut. She wasn't afraid of being captured. Outrunning them would be simple. It was their camera she feared. A shot of "werewolf girl" lurking in the ravine would make proving her harmlessness even more difficult. The damage to her RSVP list could be irreparable. Her black currant would have been wasted on the mosquitoes....

Footsteps crunched toward her. The girls were getting closer. She could hear their beating hearts. One thumped genuine curiosity—*babumbabumbabum*; the other, revenge—*ba-bum ba-bum ba-bum.*

The pair approached the tree. Leaned closer. Paused. The anticipation made Clawdeen squirm. Something was crawling up the side of her neck. It was gearing up to bite her. She let it. It itched. She imagined scratching it. It still itched. She imagined scratching it with a rake. She wondered how fast she'd have to run to become invisible.

Bekka shook a branch. Dried leaves rained down around her. "Come to mama," she cooed, clearly delighting in the thrill of intimidation. *They've found me! Now what?* "Don't be afraid. Come on." Kissy sounds popped off Bekka's thin lips like she was calling a dog. This girl was more frightening than a monster could ever be.

Haylee clapped her hands together. "Got 'em!"

Clawdeen's ears tensed. The sound of two metal objects being rubbed together filled her with panic. *Are they knives? Silver bullets?*

"Looks like they belong to that Jetta."

The keys!

"Where are you going?" asked Bekka.

"To put them on top of the car. Someone obviously lost them. Should we leave a note?"

"Gimme those," Bekka insisted.

No!

"That's the Wolfs' car." She threw the keys. They landed on Clawdeen's toes. "Ha! Let's see them escape now."

Once Bekka and Haylee were gone, Clawdeen scooped up the keys and hurried through the ravine, on her way to find Cleo. She was so excited to make contact that she almost forgot her anger. But it quickly came back when she reminded herself that the queen bee-otch was, for some strange reason, on Bekka's side.

Awooo awoooo. Reeeow reeeow. Awooo awoooo. Reeeow reeeow.

Clawdeen stood in the flower beds beneath Cleo's bedroom window, howling their secret *wolf-calling-a-cat* call. They'd used it to summon each other back in elementary school, before they got cells. That heap of stone phones at RIP told her it was probably wise to revive it.

Awooo awoooo. Reeeow reeeow. Awooo awoooo. Reeeow reeeow.

All of a sudden someone sneaked up and grabbed her from behind. The assailant smelled like amber.

"For the love of Geb, where have you been?" Cleo asked, beaming. "You've completely fallen off the grid! Wait, don't tell me you're still out of service at the Hideout."

Clawdeen took a distancing step back. "How could you do this to us?" she asked, her jeans stained with mud. "You and that normie Bekka—"

"*Ka!*" Cleo giggled, waving Clawdeen's anger away like a pesky fly. "Everyone knows I'm innocent. I cleared my name before everyone took off. But since you weren't there, I'll give you the thirty-second wrap-up. Iwantedtoshutdownthemovieso-youwouldmodelwithme. Guilty. I admit it. Bekkawasgoingto-helpmeeraseit. Guilty. Admitted. ThenIheardit wasn'tgoingtoair. Problem solved. SoIbailedonthenormie. She did the rest. I had no clue. Now can we move on?" Cleo clapped her hands, opened her arms wide, and hugged Clawdeen, who didn't have a chance to answer. Then Cleo linked arms with her friend and began strolling across the lawn as if nothing had ever happened.

And in the name of best friendship with a royal, Clawdeen knew it was best to pretend nothing had. "So everyone *left*? Where did they go?"

"Deucey went to Greece on one of Mr. D's private jets. Saying good-bye in front of my dad was double unsatisfying and triple awkward."

"Did Jackson leave too? Is that why Melody was running around in her pajamas crying the other night?"

"Ha! True, she does dress like a Snuggie model, but don't let her sleepover style fool you. That normie has some serious sass-appeal. You should have seen her scare off Bekka. It was actually kind of *weird*," Cleo said, her gold bangles jingling. "Speaking *of*, can you believe Deuce is gone?"

"So is my party if this whole thing doesn't get fixed soon."

"We promised to be exclusive, even when he's in Greece, but I can't help thinking he's met someone else. Why else wouldn't he call?"

Clawdeen speed-scratched her neck bites. "Where did Lala and Blue go? And what about Jackson? Do you think they'll come back for my birthday?"

"I'll tell you one thing." Cleo stopped strolling to look Clawdeen in the eye. The late-afternoon sun reflected off her caramel-colored streaks and brightened her topaz eyes. She might be high maintenance, but there was no denying she was beautiful. "If I don't hear from him by then, I'll be making the rounds like *Grey's Anatomy*. Exclusivity pledge or not." Cleo began strolling again and sighed. "This whole thing is a major pain in the Aswan."

Clawdeen sighed too. Having a typical free-for-all chat with Cleo felt better than a hot shower in a boy-free bathroom. It didn't matter that they weren't actually having a *conversation*; all that mattered was that they were together.

"We've got to go!" Clawd shouted, sprinting up Cleo's lawn.

He was still in his green-and-yellow football uniform, helmet under his arm. "Did you find the keys?"

Clawdeen tossed them to him.

"What keys?" Cleo asked, hating to not know the details.

"Come on, let's move," he insisted, pulling his sister by the arm. His palm was sweaty. His cheeks were flushed. He smelled like duct tape and sweat. "We have to get back to the inn."

"Why?" she whined. Now that she had Cleo back, it was even harder to leave than before.

"Coach Donnelly set me up. He was trying to trap me. A few of the guys on the team warned me before the game, so I took off. He's looking for me."

Clawdeen speed-scratched her neck again. "But we haven't even talked about centerpieces or—"

"Deenie, we have to go!" Clawd lifted her over his shoulder and began running.

"Wait!" Cleo called.

Clawdeen began hitting her brother's back. "Put me down! I want to stay!"

"We're a pack," he said, panting. "We stick together."

"I don't want to be a pack. I wanna be a lone wolf."

He set her down beside the Jetta, opened the doors, and forced her inside.

"Normies are invading Blue's house. Ours could be next!" Clawdeen tried.

"It's just a house," he said, slamming her door. He hurried to the driver's side, put the key in the ignition, and peeled away from the curb.

"What about my friends? My life is here."

"If it's *life* you want, we need to get out of here. *Fast!*"

Clawd sped toward the inn, with Clawdeen strapped into the seat next to him.

Playing it safe. Just like always.

It was Tuesday after school, and Billy stood in a wood-framed tub wearing nothing but Candace's purple-and-white-striped Victoria's Secret boy shorts. Which on him fit more like baby-boy shorts. It was either those or her scant bikini bottoms, because Beau's XL Calvins were out of the question. Billy had been working out lately, but not that much.

"Stop looking," Billy said, cheeks burning.

Candace giggled. "I'm a professional."

"Forget it." Billy stepped onto the cold lip of the tub. "I can't do this." Not even Frankie Stein was worth this kind of humiliation.

"Come on! So far, so good. Don't you want to see what the rest of you looks like?" Candace gently pushed him back into the tub.

"Not as much as you do," Billy snapped.

He looked at Candace for a moment. Even in a baggy pair of her father's old scrubs, wearing snowboard goggles and a shower cap, the girl was flawless. Not that flawless was his thing—he was more of a stitches-and-bolts kind of guy. But he admired Candace's beauty and envied her confidence, especially now, moments before discovering his own potential. What if invisible was his best option?

"Remember; arms out, mouth closed, eyes closed. Only breathe when the machine is off." Candace lowered the goggles over her eyes, stuffed a few errant blond strands under her plastic cap, and lifted what looked like a portable vacuum cleaner. "Inhale, exhale, and..." She aimed the hose at his chest, depressed the silver handle, and unleashed the tanning solution. "Arctic blast!"

Cold spray coated his chest. Billy wanted to scream, but he wasn't allowed to breathe. Thankfully, the only mirrors in the Carvers' upstairs bathroom were two small rectangles above the wood-paneled vanity: one over each basin. The tub was outside their range.

"The tan takes six hours to appear, but there's bronzer in the mixture so we can see immediate results." She turned off the hose. "Breathe."

Billy exhaled. "How does it look?"

"Like someone's been doing his crunches," Candace said, impressed. "Mouth closed, eyes closed, only breathe when the machine is off, and here we go again." Next she painted his legs, applying the spray in gentle brushstrokes, contouring and defining with the precision of a true artist. After a while Billy got used to the chilly blasts and even started to enjoy them. Each invigorating shot woke a different part of his body, yanked it off the bench, and forced it into the game.

Candace snapped off the hose, lifted her goggles, and took a step back. "Done." Her expression gave nothing away.

"Well?"

"Hmmm."

"What? What's wrong?"

"Shh. Be quiet. I'm in the zone." She tapped her chin thoughtfully. "Let's dye your hair next, put in the contacts, and then get you dressed."

The following hour was a dizzying mix of chemical smells, Rihanna and Katy Perry tracks, and contemplative *mmmm*s from Candace. Finally, she was done.

Her warm hand covered his eyes. She guided him, stumbling, into her bedroom.

"Ready?" she asked, stopping before her full-length mirror.

"Ready," he answered, lying. The instant she moved her hand, Billy's life would never be the same. He'd never be able to blame his lack of dates on anything but himself. Never get to pretend he was a chiseled god cursed to a life of loneliness. Never be able to eavesdrop or be the gossip go-to guy. He'd be fallible. Excuse-free. Normal.

"One...two...three..." Candace removed her hand. "Invisible out!"

Billy looked into her full-length mirror and gasped.

And for the first time in years, his reflection gasped back.

CHAPTER ELEVEN
GOING GAGA

Frankie draped gray muslin curtains around the glass cage. Sewed five mini beanbags out of jewel-toned fabric samples and filled them with uncooked couscous. Brightened up the saw-dust by mixing in some orange and fuchsia flower petals. And winterized the lab rats' coats by replacing their summery multi-colored glitter with shimmering coal-colored flecks. The Glitte-rati's Extreme Home Makeover was complete.

Now what?

Her homework was done. Her room was clean. Tomorrow's outfit had been selected. If she didn't come up with another distraction—*fast*—her thoughts would wander back to Brett. *His absences from school…dismissive text…heartless betrayal… denim-blue eyes…STOP!* If only she had someone to talk to. But Cleo spent most of her time with Julia and their normie friends, Melody was a no-show for the second day in a row, and

Billy wasn't an option—at least not in public. Not that missing the guy who had crushed her was something she wanted to advertise. But Frankie watched *Gossip Girl*. She knew that other girls, even rich normies, missed heartbreakers too.

Something rapped lightly against her window. *Rain again?* Soft knocks followed. *Brett?* Frankie approached slowly, hoping it might be him. Then she pinched her arm for hoping. The sharp nip was less painful than the stab of disappointment.

Something—a stick of gum?—was pressed against the frosted pane. She looked up and squinted. Her fingertips tingled. Did it say...*Gaga?*

Frankie dragged over the stepladder, climbed up, and pushed the window open. The mysterious object fell to the ground. Hanging out the window, she looked closer. *Was it really?* A ticket to the sold-out Lady Gaga concert?

OmiGaga!

She extended her arm, but the ticket moved beyond her reach. Frankie shimmied out the window and tried a second time. It moved again. She scanned the cul-de-sac for an explanation.

The leaves were still; the orange-and-navy sky, clear. It couldn't have been the wind. She bent down, and the ticket slithered away. *Is this some kind of joke? Or worse? What if it's a trap?* Earlier that day Cleo mentioned that Coach Donnelly had tried to trick Clawd. What if the coach knew about her disguise?

Am I next on his hit list?

Summoning every last ounce of willpower, Frankie turned away from the ticket and raced for the house.

"Wait!" called a familiar voice. "Frankie, it's me."

Billy?

She stopped and turned.

But the guy walking toward her, dragging the ticket by a piece of fishing wire, was sooo not Billy. For one thing, she could *see* him. For two things, he wasn't nakie. And for three things, he looked like an Abercrombie model from planet *Hot*! One step closer and her normie-colored makeup would melt.

Backing away, she noted his ability to turn a simple olive-colored tee, dark-wash Diesels, and vintage white Adidas into the best Brett distraction of the day. His wavy hair, thick-but-not-Jonas-thick brows, and almond-shaped eyes were espresso brown. His toned arms were the color of caramel; his teeth were whipped-cream white. Tempting, steamy, and out of her league, he could have been added to the menu at Starbucks. Still, Frankie continued to back away.

"Stop moving, will ya?" he said, his kind voice unmistakably Billy-like.

"But how—?"

"Candace helped me," he said, leaning against the concrete exterior of her house. The sun was dipping below the horizon. It cast a warm orange glow on the neighborhood and lit him like art. He folded his arms across his chest and smiled shyly. "So, what do you think?"

"Good." She giggled nervously.

"Good?"

Frankie sparked.

"I mean, voltage." Frankie blushed, suddenly too shy to make eye contact. Why was she wearing old pink sweats and UGGs?

And why did she care? This was Billy. Her buddy. Only he looked more like an actor who might play Billy if their lives ever became a movie. But he was still the same guy, and *that* guy didn't care what she was wearing. He never had. Why should she?

"So, are you going to register for school now?" she asked, trying to make things feel normal.

"Hmmm," he said, with a sexy half-smile. "I never thought about that." He pulled a roll of Starburst out of his side pocket and offered her one. It happened to be green. They giggled.

"So, what's it like to have a place to store things?" Frankie asked, chewing the lime-flavored candy.

"Great," he said, unwrapping a pink square. "I have all kinds of things in here." He reached into his back pocket and pulled out another ticket. "What are you doing October thirtieth?"

"They're *real*?"

He nodded.

"Really?"

Billy nodded again.

"Mint!" Frankie yelled, pulling him in for a hug. He hugged her back with every muscle in his arms. "I love that you're not nakie anymore."

"Me too," he said softly. His breath smelled like sweet strawberries.

She squeezed tighter and grinned. It was easy to stick to her own kind when her own kind looked like this.

CHAPTER TWELVE
J WALKING

Melody snapped open her locker for the first time all week. She had been living for biology ever since she said good-bye to Jackson at the coffee shop. Seeing Ms. J would help her feel connected to him. Maybe Jackson's mom would deliver a secret love note from him. Or invite Melody to meet them for another clandestine meeting, or—

"I like to be *fashionably* late, but you're, like, on *couture* time," Cleo joked, the olive-and-blue bird feathers dangling from her ears.

"Those feathers actually look cute," Melody said, slamming her locker shut.

"No trade backs," Cleo said as they merged into hallway traffic. It seemed lighter than usual. There was an overall malaise in the students they passed. Usually, the halls buzzed between classes, but today they hummed. Last week everyone bustled; now they meandered. The energy dial had been turned way down. It was life unplugged. Everything felt acoustic. "Are you *seriously* just getting here? It's last period on *Wednesday*!"

"I know." Melody sighed. "My parents are away, and it's been kind of a weird week, so..."

"Manu told me."

"He *did*?"

"Yeah, he wanted me to make sure you were okay and to find a subtle way of letting you know that families are messy and that love matters more than blood...unless, of course, you're you-know-who." She made finger-fangs and wiggled them playfully. "*Ka!* I miss that girl."

Nausea wave-pooled through Melody's insides. *Why would Manu blab my secret to a big gossip?* "You have to promise not to tell anyone."

Cleo drew an imaginary crown on her green-and-yellow sweater dress. "Crown my heart and hope to rot! Besides..." She put an amber-scented arm around Melody and pulled her close. Gold bangles jabbed into Melody's shoulder blade. "I've had mummy issues for 5,842 years. It's the last thing I want to talk about."

"What is?" Frankie asked, appearing beside them. "Come on, tell me. I have some voltage Billy gossip. I'll trade you."

Melody noted that Frankie's green skin was hidden under a turtleneck sweater, black skinny jeans, and knee-high motor-cycle boots, but her long-lost curves had definitely been found. *Did she always look like the number 8? Why suddenly show off her shape? Maybe Brett is back.*

"Mum's the word," Cleo said, giggling at her pun. "If Melody wants to talk about it, she can. I swore I wouldn't."

"Cle-o!" Melody snapped. She could have been mad, *should* have been mad, but these girls had trusted her with their lives. Why not trust them back?

"Please," Frankie begged. Her smile was electric and impossible to resist.

On the way to class, Melody filled them in on Marina. She told them about her old camel-hump nose and the unsettling glance between her so-called parents. When she was done, a memory of skinny-dipping with Candace at the Four Seasons Maui flashed through her mind. Just like that risqué plunge, this admission left her feeling both exhilarated and exposed.

"You're not upset, are you?" Frankie asked, as if Melody had been mourning a chipped nail.

"Of course I am," Cleo snapped. "Deuce is my *boyfriend*. He should have called by now."

Frankie giggled. "I'm talking about the mama drama."

"Of course I'm upset," Melody said. "My parents have been lying to me. And now I have no idea who I am or where I came from. It's creepy."

"More creepy than sleeping in a laboratory with wires clamped to your neck?" Frankie mumbled from the side of her mouth.

"Or spending a few millennia alone in a dark sarcophagus?"

"Um…" Melody had no idea how to respond without offending them.

"We all have freaky parents, and we all come from freaky places," Cleo said while checking out the passing students. "Get over it."

"I think she meant your parents love you and that's all that matters," Frankie tried, flashing her contagiously perky smile.

114

Melody couldn't help smiling back. "Yeah, I'm sure that's *exactly* what she meant."

"Okay, ready for my Billy gossip?" Frankie asked.

"*Ka!*" Cleo pulled down a poster that had been taped to the cinder-block wall. It announced "sudden openings" on the school's football, basketball, and swim teams and urged students of "all fitness levels" to try out. "All the cool people are gone."

"Present company excluded, right?" Frankie asked.

Ignoring her, Cleo took a wad of pink gum from her mouth and stuck it onto a locker. "There are anti-RAD rallies every morning and monster jokes written in the bathroom stalls. Classes are half empty."

"Oh, and you should see the cafeteria," Frankie said to Melody. "You know the lunchtime playlist? 'Imagine' was on it. You know, by John Legend."

"You mean John Lennon?" Melody giggled.

"Cleo!" Frankie swatted her on the arm. "You told me his last name was Legend."

"Oops." Cleo smirked. "My bad."

"Anyway," Frankie continued, "the list was all peace songs."

"So some people have been supportive?" Melody asked as they climbed the stairs to the second floor.

"Yeah, but not enough," Cleo said as two overly buff twelfth-grade guys started down the steps wearing matching T-shirts. RAD was spray-painted across the front in black letters, but the R was crossed out and replaced with a B.

Frankie rolled her periwinkle-blue eyes. "Real clever."

"What did you expect?" Melody muttered. "A smart idiot?"

Suddenly, three girls wearing pirate masks and wielding prop swords appeared behind them, pushing past students, knocking over books. Melody recognized her sister.

"Seize them!" Candace called. Some students reached out to grab the guys; others stepped aside and let them pass. Casually, Cleo stuck out her foot. The boys tripped down the last two steps but quickly righted themselves and made a move for the first-floor hallway.

"Stop!" Melody ordered.

The two boys halted, like a video being paused.

Whoa!

"Golden," Cleo exclaimed.

"Mint!" Frankie added.

Melody felt as if everyone in the stairwell was staring at her.

"Attack!" Candace shouted. Her fellow pirates pounced on the guys like spider monkeys and began slicing off their shirts with dull sabers.

"What's going on?" Cleo whispered to Melody. "Why is everyone listening to you lately?"

Thankfully, Principal Weeks broke up the skirmish before Melody could answer. Not that she didn't want to. She just didn't know how.

Ms. J was late for class. Her chair was one of five left empty in the lab. Despite the restless chatter and bursts of laughter, those who were missing stood out the most.

Frankie leaned forward and whispered, "Have you seen Billy?"

"Is that supposed to be funny?" Cleo asked, not bothering to turn around.

Melody giggled.

"No, I'm serious," Frankie said. "This is what I've been trying to tell you. Mel's sister gave him a makeover. He's megawatt hot."

"I was wondering what Billy and Candace were doing in the bathroom for so long," Melody said, checking the door for Ms. J.

"He's taking me to see Lady Gaga," Frankie said, beaming.

"Does this mean you're over Brett?" Melody asked.

"Who?"

"Brett."

"Who?" Frankie smiled. And then she squealed, "Ah!" Rubbing the back of her neck, she turned to face Bekka — and the red barrel of a squirt gun. "What was that for?" Frankie asked.

"Science experiment. They say water and electricity don't mix, but you seem just fine — *Frankie Stein*."

Her snooty friends giggled. Melody couldn't imagine how Frankie was dealing with the assault and was too mortified to check. Instead, she picked her cuticles and prayed for Ms. J to show up soon.

Thomp. A clove of garlic hit the side of Melody's head and bounced to the floor. Muffled snickers followed.

"Looks like we can cross vampire off the list," Bekka called from the back of the room. Dressed in a red and pink flower-print dress, she appeared deceptively sweet as she sat on her desk, swinging her legs.

Haylee dutifully drew a line through something in her pink composition notebook.

Next, Cleo got whacked in the cheek with a brown biscuit. "Ow!" She picked up the biscuit and whipped it back.

"No dog would turn down a Milk-Bone," Bekka said. "Cross off werewolf."

Haylee did.

"Werewolves are not *dogs*!" Cleo stood and began unclipping her earrings.

"Ignore her," Frankie muttered.

Cleo set the feathers on her desk and told Melody, "They're yours if anything happens to me."

Is she really going to fight? Because the last thing RADs needed was normie blood on their hands.

"Sit," Melody insisted.

Cleo did.

"Ha! Good trick." Bekka clapped her hands. "Looks like she is a dog, after all."

More laughter from the back of the room.

"You're the *dog*," Cleo said. "That's why Brett ditched you for Frankie."

The room was silent. Bekka and Frankie were probably on the verge of tears. After all, Brett had left them both.

"Why are you on *their* side all of a sudden?" Bekka asked Cleo.

"All of a *sudden*? Please, I've been on their side my whole life," Cleo fired back with a little too much conviction.

Bekka lifted her eyebrow. *"Really?"*

"I mean, the side where people can do what they want. The anti-mean side."

"Interesting." Bekka began strolling toward Cleo, arms behind her back like a puffed-up prosecutor. "Then why," she asked, stopping at Cleo's desk, "were you so into destroying their little documentary?"

Melody's heart revved. Bekka had Michael Moore's passion for exposing people. One slipup from Cleo was all she needed.

Melody stood too and approached Bekka. They were so close that Melody could smell the other girl's mango-scented lip gloss. "Why don't you just admit it?"

"Admit *what*?" Bekka asked, blinking.

"That *you*'re a monster."

"*Me*?" Bekka scoffed.

"Yeah, a green-eyed monster!" Frankie giggled, completing Melody's thought.

"Ha! Golden!" Cleo lifted her palm. The three girls high-fived. A tiny spark passed between them. Frankie quickly stuffed her hands back into her jeans pockets.

Bekka rolled her eyes. "And who would I be jealous of, Melody? *You*? Because you're dating some bipolar guy who's allergic to his own sweat?"

"No. You're jealous of Frankie, and you're making everyone suffer because of it," Melody said. "This whole monster hunt is about your bruised ego."

"'Scuse me?" Bekka retorted, hands on her hips.

"You need someone to blame because Brett's not into you

anymore. So you're going after innocent people." Melody shook with conviction. "Just admit it."

Bekka's blinking eyes darkened to the color of summer storm clouds. "Fine, I admit it."

Cleo smacked her desk. "Nice!"

Confused glances shot up and down the rows.

Huh?

"I knew it!" Frankie said.

"Do that again," Cleo urged Melody.

Melody swallowed hard and then asked, "Bekka, do you have any proof that the RADs are dangerous? Have you ever seen them hurt anyone?"

Bekka blinked again. "Yes, me! I was hurt when the green girl kissed Brett." Her freckly cheeks flushed, and her eyes teared.

"I mean *physically*," Melody demanded.

Bekka shook her head.

"Are you *kidding* me?" Haylee called, tearing a page out of her notebook and crumpling it up.

"Of course I am," Bekka said, managing a smile.

"Are you?" Melody pressed.

Bekka lowered her head. "No."

How am I doing this?

"Do you know where Brett is?" Frankie tried.

Bekka leaned against an empty desk and folded her arms. "Of course I do."

Frankie stood, her hands deep in her pockets. "Tell me."

"He doesn't want you to know. He only wants me to know."

"So you've been talking to him?" Frankie asked.

Bekka twirled her *B* charm necklace. "Yup."

"Do you *really* know where Brett is?" Melody pressed.

Bekka sighed. "No."

"Have you been talking to him?"

"No."

"Case dismissed!"

Murmurs built to mumbles. Bekka hurried back toward her friends to appeal.

"Wait, I have one more question," Melody announced.

Everyone stopped talking.

"This one is for Haylee."

The mousy girl pushed her beige glasses up her wide nose and then nodded that she was ready.

"Why do you let Bekka boss you around?"

The defendant's brown eyes shifted from her old master to the new one.

"Hay-leeee," Bekka warned. "Don't answer."

"You have to," Melody insisted.

Haylee began blinking.

"Tell me," Melody said.

Bekka shook her head. Haylee nodded. And then, "I signed one of her indentured-service contracts in eighth grade. It doesn't expire until sophomore year of college."

A few of the students laughed at the idea, but Melody flashed back to the loyalty contract Bekka had made her sign on the first day of school. What was it about high school that made people think with their insecurities instead of their brains?

"Did you ever try to break it?" Melody asked.

"Eleven times. It's tight. Her father drafted it." Haylee reached inside her green crocodile-skin attaché case and pulled out a legal document. She held it out in front of her, offering it to Melody.

"Destroy it," Melody ordered Bekka, who quickly swooped in and tore it to bits.

"Does this mean I'm free?" Haylee asked.

Bekka threw the paper at her ex-friend. It covered her like confetti on Independence Day.

"Us too?" asked one of their friends.

"All of you," Bekka shouted, her face ablaze with humiliation. "You're the reason Brett broke up with me, anyway."

"*Us?*" asked Haylee.

"Yeah. He was embarrassed to be seen with you!" Bekka hugged her books to her chest like a shield.

"Why?" asked a girl with chipmunk cheeks. "What did *we* do?"

"Britt, skinny jeans are for skinny people! Deelya, close your mouth when you breathe! Rachel, either pop those whiteheads or build a chairlift on your face and sell season passes! Morgan, you smell like Kraft Singles. And Haylee, you dress like my nana. Why do you think Heath never asked you out?"

"Because he can't stand *you*!"

Haylee lifted the green case over her head and turned it upside down. Contracts fell like paratroopers jumping to freedom. Britt, Deelya, Rachel, and Morgan ripped their way to happiness.

"You're all dead to me!" Bekka shouted. She gathered her things and stomped toward the door amid mounting chaos. On the way out, she collided with a grape-shaped woman wearing a paisley-print sweater set and navy slacks. "And where are you going?" asked the stranger, righting the Whole Foods tote bag that had slipped off her shoulder.

"To a normal school!" Bekka barked before taking off down the hall.

Everyone began applauding. Frankie joy-kicked the back of Melody's chair while the grape worked to restore order.

Cleo leaned across the row and whispered, "Spill. How are you doing that?"

Melody searched for an answer but came up short. "I just ask and—"

"No," Cleo said, plucking an olive, blue, and gold feather from Melody's hair. She twirled it between her fingers, admiring its iridescent sheen. "Where are these coming from? I could design a whole jewelry collection around them." She held it to her collarbone. "Perfect with my earrings, right?"

Melody reached out her hand, testing her power of persuasion on the most stubborn subject of all. "Kiss it good-bye and give it to me."

Cleo blinked, kissed the feather, and tucked it behind Melody's ear.

"Earrings too."

Without hesitation, Cleo did what she'd been told.

Manu was right, Melody realized. Her voice was irresistible.

"Sorry I'm late. I was in a meeting with Principal Weeks," announced the grape. "My name is Mrs. Stern-Figgus. I'll be taking over for Ms. J."

Melody's stomach lurched.

"Where is she?" asked Britt.

The round woman turned to the blackboard and began writing her name. "I wasn't given that information."

Of course you were. "Where is Ms. J?" Melody tried.

"She was forced to resign," said Mrs. Stern-Figgus.

Several students gasped.

"By Principal Weeks?" Melody pressed.

"School board."

"Why?"

The teacher turned around. "Harboring a RAD." She blinked.

Not just a RAD! Her son! What's wrong with these people?

"Where is she now?" asked Melody, voice quaking.

Mrs. Stern-Figgus shrugged. Of course she didn't know. Melody didn't even know, and Jackson was her boyfriend. Were they leaving? Were they gone? Was there time to stop them? All this time wasted in class, toying with Bekka, when she could have been out looking for them.

Melody stood and grabbed her books. Everyone in the class was staring. She couldn't have cared less.

"What is this, Grand Central Station? Where is everyone running off to? Where are you going, Miss..." The teacher snapped her fingers.

"Carver. Melody Carver. And I'm not sure where I'm going."

Cleo and Frankie giggled. Maybe some of the others did too. It was hard to hear with all that panic ringing in her ears.

Mrs. Stern-Figgus clapped twice. "Sit down."

"I can't. I have to go."

"Do you have a permission slip?"

Stepping into the hallway, Melody said, "No. So when you take attendance, please mark me down as present."

Mrs. Stern-Figgus flashed an agreeable thumbs-up and then waved good-bye.

Melody didn't stick around to bask in the approval of her classmates. Instead, she clipped on her earrings, secured the feather behind her ear, and hurried outside. She was finally ready for the truth. All she had to do was ask and brace herself for the answer. And this time she would get it.

TO: (503) 555-5474
oct 21, 3:07 PM
BRETT: I TOLD YOU I DON'T WANT TO TALK. STOP STALKING ME.

TO: Brett
oct 21, 3:08 PM
(503) 555-5474: NOT STALKING YOU. MOVED ON.

TO: (503) 555-5474
oct 21, 3:09 PM
BRETT: THEN WHAT'S WITH THE CHANNEL 2 NEWS TRUCK PARKED IN FRONT OF MY HOUSE?

TO: Brett
oct 21, 3:09 PM
(503) 555-5474: DUNNO. ASK THEM!

TO: (503) 555-5474
oct 21, 3:10 PM
BRETT: WHO ARE YOU? CHANNEL 4?

TO: Brett
oct 21, 3:10 PM
(503) 555-5474: NO CHANNEL!!!!

TO: (503) 555-5474
oct 21, 3:11 PM
BRETT: WHO THEN?

TO: Brett
oct 21, 3:11 PM
(503) 555-5474: UH, FRANKIE. REMEMBER ME?

TO: (503) 555-5474
oct 21, 3:12 PM
BRETT: STEIN??????

TO: Brett
oct 21, 3:12 PM
(503) 555-5474: Y. WHO DID U THINK IT WAS?

TO: (503) 555-5474
oct 21, 3:13 PM
BRETT: REPORTERS. WHAT NUMBER IS THIS???

TO: Brett
oct 21, 3:13 PM
(503) 555-5474: NEW PHONE. LONG STORY.

TO: Frankie
oct 21, 3:14 PM
BRETT: BEEN CALLING UR OLD NUMBER FOR DAYS. GOES STRAIGHT TO VOICE MAIL. I THOUGHT YOU HATED ME.

TO: Brett
oct 21, 3:15 PM
FRANKIE: WHERE HAVE YOU BEEN?

TO: Frankie
oct 21, 3:16 PM
BRETT: PORTLAND. HIDING AT COUSIN'S CUZ PRESS HAS BEEN HOUNDING ME. AT MY HOUSE 24/7. BEKKA'S GONNA PAY FOR THIS.

TO: Brett
oct 21, 3:16 PM
FRANKIE: ALREADY HAS. ☺

TO: Frankie
oct 21, 3:17 PM
BRETT: U AROUND SATURDAY? I CAN TAKE THE TRAIN. MEET U HALFWAY.

TO: Frankie
oct 21, 3:19 PM
BRETT: JUST CHECKED. ONLY $7 PER TICKET.

TO: Frankie
oct 21, 3:21 PM
BRETT: TAKE THE 11:22 AM FROM SALEM STATION. GET OFF IN OREGON CITY. MEET U THERE. LAST BENCH ON THE PLATFORM.

TO: Frankie
oct 21, 3:23 PM
BRETT: OK?

TO: Frankie
oct 21, 3:24 PM
BRETT: U STILL THERE?

TO: Frankie
oct 21, 3:25 PM
BRETT: I'LL BRING SALTWATER TAFFY. MY COUSIN OWNS A CANDY SHOP. ☺

TO: Brett
oct 21, 3:25 PM
FRANKIE: K. BUT LET'S KEEP IT BETWEEN US FOR NOW. YOU KNOW, FOR SAFETY.

TO: Frankie
oct 21, 3:25 PM
BRETT: SMART. SEE U SATURDAY.

TO: Brett
oct 21, 3:26 PM
FRANKIE: DON'T FORGET THE TAFFY. ☺

TO: Frankie
oct 21, 3:27 PM
BRETT: I WON'T. ☺ BTW WERE YOU SERIOUS ABOUT "MOVING ON"?

TO: Frankie
oct 21, 3:28 PM
BRETT: HELLO?

TO: Frankie
oct 21, 3:29 PM
BRETT: U THERE?

TO: Frankie
oct 21, 3:30 PM
BRETT: FRANKIE?

LOST CHAPTER
(WHOSE UNLUCKY NUMBER SHALL GO UNMENTIONED)

CHAPTER FOURTEEN
MEAT, PRAY, LOVE

Nino aimed the camera at his sister. His stringy black hair fell in front of the lens, but he quickly tucked it behind his ear. "And...action!" he called.

More than a cue, the word had become Clawdeen's only hope for surviving her first week of captivity. No more sulking around the inn, begging her brothers for driving lessons, or doing thousand-piece granny-loving kitten puzzles while mourning the inevitable death of her party. If she wanted to make a name for herself in the cutthroat world of DIY decorating, she'd have to beef up her blog. And so she enlisted her youngest brother, swiped the key to suite 9, and got to work.

"Hi, I'm Clawdeen Wolf," she announced with a confident smile. "Welcome to another episode of Where There's a Wolf, There's a Way..." It was the fifth one she'd shot that week. Not that her seven loyal followers would know. Like her, they would be kept in the dark until life returned to normal and she had access to a computer. But when that time came, they would not be disappointed.

"I was hired to upgrade this hotel room from drab to fab using nothing but construction scraps and my own creative flair."

Nino snickered. Probably because he knew how opposite of *hired* she really was and how opposite of *alive* she would be if she couldn't restore the room to its original state before her parents found out.

Three days earlier, the understated rustic retreat had been furnished with pine-green accents, raw-wood furniture, and a king-sized bed covered with a red and royal blue Navajo blanket. Now, Friday night, the space was well on its way to becoming the Sweet Suite—the must-have room for the eighteen-and-under crowd.

Broken glassware from the kitchen had been glued to the mini-fridge in a colorful mosaic that spelled EAT; above the bathtub the mosaic said CHILL, and behind the bed she'd written REST. Old coffee tins had been covered in fur (thanks, boys) and dyed purple to play up the faux facade. In the cans, Clawdeen displayed hairbrushes, makeup brushes, pens, and even beef jerky. Old hardcover books "borrowed" from the inn's library had been stacked and shellacked with glossy, high-fashion photos, transforming them into bedside pillars. One displayed fashion dos; the other, don'ts. The family's old CD collection, stored at the inn for guests who doubted the staying power of iTunes, had finally been put to use. Clawdeen glued the discs to the wooden walls, reflective side showing, to give guests the sense that they were sleeping inside a disco ball—because who didn't want that?

"Tonight," Clawdeen continued, "I'm going to teach you how to transform an entire Polly Pocket doll collection into a chandelier, or a chan-*doll*-ier, as I like to call it."

She padded over the soon-to-be-covered-in-glitter rug and stopped at the desk. It was strewn with cable wires, tiny figurines, and spools of metallic string. Nino followed. "Before you get started, it's very important that you—"

Suddenly, Clawdeen's ears tightened. Music thumped in the distance.

"Stand by," Nino said, lowering the camera.

Clawdeen checked her reflection while they waited for the disruption to pass. The moon was filling out, and with it came the usual warning signs that transformation was approaching. Her auburn hair and nails had grown at least half an inch since lunch. Her metabolism was firing, making the tight aubergine minidress she had put on an hour earlier loose around the waist. And her yellow-brown eyes radiated fierce passion. Funny, every TV hostess in Hollywood would sell her soul for those traits, and yet she was the one hiding.

The music was getting closer. People were singing, their voices muffled, like they were inside a car. Ke$ha's "We R Who We R" was blasting at full volume. Clawdeen held her breath and listened to the long-lost sounds of fun.

"They're pulling in," Nino said, rushing to the window. "Look!"

A black Escalade pulled up the drive. Typical self-centered

normie behavior—assuming the SORRY sign applied to everyone else but them. If they only knew that the woman making their creamed spinach wore a hairnet over her entire body.

Inside the SUV, two voices wailed: *"We'll be forever young!"*

Clawdeen sang along. *"We are who we are."* She knew every word. How could she not? Lala played it in her car every morning on their way to—*Omigod!* She tossed the suite key to Nino. "That's a wrap. Lock up, will ya?"

Clawdeen charged down the forest-green carpeted staircase and rushed out to greet the SUV.

The windows were fogged—probably from the blasting heat—but Clawdeen didn't hesitate. She pulled open the driver's door and jumped inside. Lala and her uncle Vlad were dancing in their seats, waving their arms above their heads and belting out the final chorus.

"Deenie!" Lala threw herself into Clawdeen's open arms. Apart for only a week, they hugged as though it had been forever.

"I know when I'm not wanted," joked Uncle Vlad, leaning over his niece to shut off the ignition. "Guess I'll make like under-eye cream and get the bags."

Lala's fangs began chattering as the heat escaped through the open door. Her gray fedora, yellow hoodie, black satin blazer, leggings, and knee-high boots obviously weren't enough to keep her warm on a sixty-seven-degree night. And it looked as if she hadn't eaten for days.

"Bags?" Clawdeen asked. "What bags? What are you doing here? Where have you been?"

"Can we talk about it inside?" Lala asked, grabbing a couple of parasols from the backseat. "It's cold out here in the sticks."

"What's going on out here?" Clawd asked from the doorway. "Mom's been calling you for dinner. Where's Nino?" He was wearing his football jersey for the same reason Clawdeen had painted her nails in green glitter polish and enhanced them with silver bow stickers: hope.

"Look who's here!" Clawdeen announced, rub-warming her friend's delicate arms as they entered the inn.

"Lala," Clawd said, his expression softening from watchdog to puppy dog.

"Fresh off the plane from Romania!" She slapped him five, jammed her parasols into the steel umbrella holder, and hurried into the warm lobby.

Candlelit and cozy, it was a balanced mix of log cabin and Henry VIII. The granite registration desk was flanked by dark walnut walls covered in black-and-white photos of castles. Navy wingback chairs, a Scotch plaid sofa, and an iron coffee table faced a stone fireplace. Bookshelves offered classic novels and sun-bleached board games. Lala went straight for the hearth and held her hands to the flames.

"Romania?" Clawdeen asked. "With the grimparents?"

"Yup, Dad forced me. He thought I'd be safe there. Funny thing is, I almost died of starvation. The closest thing to a vegetable that Grumpma served was sausage from a corn-fed pig."

"Where do you want these?" Uncle Vlad panted as he dragged

two massive trunks into the foyer. Old, worn, and wheelless, they could have been recovered from the *Titanic*.

"Wait, you're staying?" Clawdeen asked.

"Sur-priiiise!" Lala singsonged.

"I'll get those," Clawd said. With a small grunt, he stacked the trunks and lifted them over his head. "I'll put them in Deenie's room." He began climbing the stairs.

Uncle Vlad pulled a hankie from the pocket of his teal-checked blazer and dabbed his slick forehead. "Show-off."

"We have tons of room," Clawdeen offered. "I'm sure my mom won't care."

"It was her idea, actually," Lala said.

"Really?"

"Our phones were taken away, and I didn't have your number. So I called the inn and she answered. All she had to do was ask how I was doing and that was it. I started bawling. My grimparents were waiting in the car, honking, because we were going on a double date. Them, me, and some fruit bat they wanted to fix me up with. Are you ready? His name was *Marian*—"

Clawd snickered from the second-floor landing.

"I called Uncle Vlad first, but—"

"Poor thing was in puddles when I picked up," he said, helping himself to a Jolly Rancher from the candy dish at the reception desk. "And I just knew. I grew up with those two. Crying was my cardio. But I'd accepted a decorating job for a five-star seafood restaurant in Portland where—get this—Demi Lovato is part owner...or is it Demi Moore?"

"So your mom said I could stay here until he gets back. I told her not to tell you. Wanted it to be a surprise."

"Fur real?" Clawdeen shrieked. *A friend! A girl! A cohost! A driving teacher! A miracle!*

Lala nodded and they squealed again.

After a round of good-bye hugs for Uncle Vlad, the girls made their way to dinner.

Clawdeen couldn't wait to fill Lala in on everything that had been happening. To hear stories about Lala's crazy relatives, laugh their way to stronger abs, and stay up all night gossiping. Lala could teach her how to drive. Assist with the Sweet Suite. And help her plan the Sassy...just in case.

The thrill of a weeklong slumber party must have tickled Lala too. Not one for silly humor, she approached the suit of armor—which held the inn's menus with its metal fingers—and smacked its butt.

"Ooh, me next!" Howie teased from the table, already eating.

"I suggest you use gloves," Don joked.

"The kind they use at the zoo to clean the elephant cages," Nino said, sitting.

"Why would he need gloves to touch the knight's butt?" Rocks wondered.

"Not him," Don said, frustrated. *"Lala."*

"Why would Lala need gloves? She just did it, and her hands are fine." Rocks smirked, stabbing a meatball.

Everyone burst out laughing—even Clawdeen, who was *so* over Rocks's airhead comments. Having Lala there definitely lightened her mood and made her feel safe in a way her brothers never could.

Like a waitress refilling her cherry Coke before she had to ask. Clawdeen finally felt like someone had her back.

"Are they being pigs?" Clawd asked, entering behind them. The wrinkled football jersey and gray sweats had been replaced by a black tee, skinny jeans, a leather belt, and sneakers. He had even spent some quality time with a comb. Hair gathered in a neat ponytail and smelling like Clawdeen's black-currant body wash, he was suddenly more fox than wolf.

The boys whistled. Lala's dark eyes gave him a once-over. Clawdeen asked if he was sneaking out later to meet a girl.

"Relax," he said, sitting. "I was fixing the clogged tub and I fell in, so I changed."

A round of accusations followed about who should be blamed for the latest plumbing issues.

"Welcome, Lala!" Harriet called, emerging from the kitchen with a steaming casserole dish. "Macaroni and cheese, just for you." Her toned triceps bulged as she set the dish down. Removing her oven mitts, she pulled Lala in for a hug. "I'm going to fatten you up," she promised. Her cheeks, flushed from cooking, matched her cinnamon-colored hair.

"I can't wait," Lala said, digging in. "I'm starving." She looked healthier already.

Harriet sat. "You look nice," she told Clawd. "I can finally see your eyes. Now if you could get Nino to—"

"No way," said the youngest, covering his head with a red napkin.

"Why? Look how handsome your brother looks."

"Don't get used to it, Mom," Clawd said, grabbing a roll from the bread basket. "It's not like this is my new look or anything. I like my hair. I just did this—"

"I bet you'd look cool with a mohawk," Lala said, lifting the scalding casserole to her lips. "They're everywhere in Romania. My cousin gave one to her boyfriend, and he looked hot. I can do it for you if you want."

"We'll see," Clawd said, grinning shyly.

Lala smiled, fangs exposed.

"So, Cleo texted me today," Clawdeen said. "She said everyone is talking about my Sassy. Even the normies."

"It's still happening?" Lala asked.

"Thank you!" Howie dropped his fork and clapped his hands. "Finally, a girl with a brain around here."

"It's eight days away," Clawdeen explained to Lala, ignoring her pompous brother. "This whole thing could be over by then."

"That's true," Lala said, returning to her food.

Clawdeen knew her friend too well. Lala didn't believe the party would happen any more than her brother did. Still, she acted as if it could, and that meant everything. It meant there was hope.

CHAPTER FIFTEEN
RAD TO THE BONE

"Truth or dare?" Melody asked, her hair adorned in blue and olive feathers.

Candace dog-eared a page in her *Marie Claire* magazine and sat up on her bed. "Dare, Kemosabe."

Pulling back the powder-pink curtains, Melody peered across the street at Jackson's cottage. Dark and lifeless. Just as it had been all week. "Pick truth."

"Okay, truth."

The game was borderline amoral, considering Candace was under the influence of Melody's spell—assuming there *was* a spell and she wasn't lying in a ditch somewhere experiencing a coma-induced hallucination. But come on, how else was she supposed to rationalize this? Melody Carver had never been the girl people listened to. Now suddenly she was calling the shots. Maybe this was some real-life version of *Freaky Friday*. Had she and Candace switched bodies? Melody glanced at her flattish chest. Not likely. Maybe one of the RADs had given her this *gift*. But who? Vampires, werewolves, zombies, mummies, gorgons... She ran through the list of everyone she knew. None of them were capable of that. The only thing that made sense (sort of) was that Melody had somehow become an overly persuasive, feather-shedding RAD. But what kind? The Black Swan?

"Where is Mom's white silk tunic?" she asked Candace, continuing to test her power.

Her sister began blinking. "You mean the tunic *formerly* known as white?"

"I guess so. Why? What happened to it?"

"Salsa happened to it at Carmen Dederich's pool party. So I dyed it black, and it actually looks better than before." Satisfied, she sank back into her down-filled pillows and returned to her magazine.

They had been playing this for almost an hour. Candace always picked dare, and then Melody, with the help of her new-found power, demanded truth. So far she had already uncovered the following information:

1. Candace loves Melody's new feather obsession. And *really* loves that her sister is exploring her personal style. But feathers and hoodies are the toothpaste and orange juice of fashion. One had to go, and Candace was rooting for the sweats.

2. When she wants to land a new crush, Candace e-mails him a JPEG of herself in a bikini. When the boy writes back,

and he always does, she says her assistant messed up—the photo was meant for her modeling agent, not him. A date request always follows.

3. Candace's diary—filled with descriptions of lonely nights spent at the library while her friends are out partying—is a fake. Left in the living room by "accident," it's intended to be read by snooping parents while she is out partying with her friends.

4. All Candace's new Salem friends think her father is a CIA operative. If they knew he was a plastic surgeon, they'd assume her beauty was enhanced. And it's not.

5. Her sciatic nerve was never pinched. The real reason she quit ballet? She tooted during a brisé and everyone heard.

6. Her biggest confession? After being forced to turn down Lori Sherman's pony party to hear Melody perform "Hirtenruf-Auf der Alp" in a yodeling recital, Candace had tossed a penny into the theater's fountain and wished away her sister's singing voice. One month later Melody developed asthma. Since then Candace had blamed herself, refusing to touch another penny as long as she lived. Hearing Melody sing at the *Teen Vogue* shoot was a huge relief. Candace no longer holds herself responsible but still refuses to touch pennies because they're worthless and dirty.

However unscrupulous this game, the distraction was necessary to calm Melody's nerves. Between Jackson's impending departure and her deceptive parents' momentary return, she had paced a landing strip in Candace's sheepskin rug.

For the previous two days, she had searched for Ms. J and Jackson. She'd asked teachers, students, and neighbors; scoured the Riverfront; flashed their pictures at airport ticket counters. Each of her subjects blinked before answering. They were telling the truth but had nothing to tell.

Beau and Glory, however, would have plenty to spill. And she was finally ready to hear it. *Ignorance is bliss* was bull. Melody had been ignorant her whole life, and things were far from blissful. It was time to give *knowledge is power* a try. "Truth or dare—"

Headlights streaked the bedroom walls. Candace tossed her magazine. "Omigod, they're home."

Melody's palms began to perspire. "Knowledge" was pulling into the driveway.

"Truth," Candace said. "Are you going to tell Mom and Dad that I used the cleaning-lady money to buy a spray-tan machine?"

"That depends. Are you planning to tell them I skipped school?"

"Never," Candace said, crossing her cami.

Melody extended her hand and they shook. "Then we have a deal."

"Ew, melting much?" Candace wiped her hand on her wine-colored skinny jeans. "Botox treats sweating, you know. You should talk to Mom and Dad about it."

"I'll add it to my list of topics."

"Hola señoritas," Beau called. *"Mamá y papá están en la casa!"*

Candace ran down the stairs and greeted them with a hug. Melody walked. Stale airplane smells clung to their matching turquoise *camisetas*.

"How was it?" Candace asked.

They giggled like spring breakers with an inside joke. *"Lo que haiga pasado en* Punta Mita *se queda en* Punta Mita," Glory said.

An expression from ten years ago should have stayed in ten years ago, Melody would have joked, but she was busy waking her courage from a fifteen-year slumber.

"Notice anything different about the house?" Candace stepped aside so they could admire her work.

"No," Beau said, not bothering to look.

"Ex-actly!" She beamed. "Everything is perfect. So feel free to go away and leave me in charge whenever you want."

"Good to know," Glory said, fanning her tanned forehead with the brim of her straw visor. "Has it always been so *caliente* in here, or am I going through the change?" She stepped down to the sunken living room and opened the doors to the ravine.

Cool air lured them to the couch, where Beau kicked off his black man-dals and reclined. *"Beaking* of the change, what's with the bird feathers, Melly?"

Candace laughed.

Glory lifted her husband's arm and nuzzled up to his chest. "Joke all you want, Beau, but that look is trending right now," she said. "It makes one look very regal."

145

"You mean *seagull*," Beau said, high-fiving Candace.

"It's nice to see you embracing fashion, Melly," Glory said. "But if you want some motherly advice, I suggest losing the hoodie and going for a fitted denim top or black cashmere."

"Thanks, but shouldn't motherly advice be coming from my *mother*?" Melody blurted.

"Me-owie," Candace purred.

Glory lifted her head off Beau's chest. Botox kept her from looking shocked, but her tone couldn't hide it. "What is *that* supposed to mean?"

"You seriously have no idea?" Melody asked. "Because I haven't been able to think about anything else all week."

"Oh yeah." Candace propped a pillow under her head and rubbed her palms together. "This is getting gooooood."

Melody turned to her sister. "Will you please go in the kitchen and get me some water?"

Candace began blinking and then stood. "With plea-sha."

Beau watched his daughter skip into the kitchen. "Is she really doing it?"

"Yup," Melody said, as if Candace had spent a lifetime taking orders from her baby sister.

Her parents exchanged a confused glance.

Melody's heart beat up a gale so mighty it forced out her words before she had time to finesse them. "Glory Carver, are you my mother?"

Glory began blinking. "Yes, Melody, I am."

Hmmm.

"Okay, then are you my *birth* mother?"

"Melly..." Beau murmured, pulling Glory in close.

She blinked more.

"Are you? Are you my birth mother?" Melody pressed.

Glory twirled her silver gift shop bangles and whispered, "No."

Glass shattered against the floor. Everyone turned. Candace, green eyes wide and spray-tanned skin pale, stood by the couch surrounded by crystal shards and water. "What did you just say?"

"It wasn't supposed to happen like this," Glory claimed. Beau squeezed her shoulders.

"We knew we'd have to discuss this eventually," he murmured into his wife's auburn hair. Her narrow shoulders shook.

Now what? Melody had spent all week anticipating her reaction to this worst-case scenario. Now that she was living it, the only thing she felt was stunned.

"Did you give birth to *me*?" Candace asked.

Glory lifted her tear-soaked face and nodded.

"Sweet!" Candace blurted. And then to Melody, "I mean, whatever. Either way is fine with me."

"Candace *out*." Melody pointed to the stairs.

"Guh-ladly," her sister said, taking them two at a time.

Melody felt gauzy and light. Ignoring her mother's aversion to smudges, she sat on the glass coffee table instead of the couch. It was too soon to share furniture.

"So, who am I?"

"You're our daughter," Beau said lovingly. "You always have been."

Hugging her knees to her chest, Melody studied her toes and wondered who had made them. "Do you know my birth parents?"

147

"No," Glory answered. "We adopted you from an agency when you were three months old. We love you just as much as Candace and—"

"Why wasn't *she* adopted?"

Glory looked at Melody, her mouth half open and ready to answer, but no words came out.

Beau ran a hand through his dark hair and sighed.

"Tell me."

"When your sister was born," he began, "she was this perfect-looking little baby...."

Why do all of his Candace stories start that way?

"We created perfection on our first try and..." He paused, considering his next words. "And I was afraid."

"Of what?" Melody asked.

"Of not being able—" His voice snagged on emotion.

"He was afraid—" Glory broke off, then started again. "We were both afraid that next time we wouldn't be so lucky. So we agreed to have only one child. And then we, you know..."

Melody shook her head. She didn't.

"We closed the family business," Glory said.

"What business?" Melody asked.

Her mother air-scissored her fingers toward Beau.

Oh.

Glory sighed. "One year later we regretted it."

"So we adopted," Beau said with a clap of his hands. "And thanks to you, we got perfection twice."

Melody knew he meant it. She never questioned their love, just their honesty.

"It was an absolute miracle," Glory began with a nostalgic grin. "We had been working with Small World Adoptions, and it was taking forever. Then one afternoon in July—I had just won the singles tennis tournament at the club, and your father got his first celebrity client—a letter arrived from the Achelous Agency. It said they'd found the perfect baby."

"I thought you were working with Small World."

"We were," Glory said. "I assumed it was a referral. So we signed the papers and took you home the next day."

"They didn't tell you anything about my mother at all? Anything having to do with her voice, or feathers, or her name?"

"Nothing other than that she had named you Melody," Beau said. "I suppose we could have pushed for more details, but we were so happy to have you that we didn't want to do anything that might change her mind. Besides, from that moment on you were ours. Where you'd come from didn't matter."

To you.

"So that whole thing about wanting to name me Melanie but Mom had a cold and the nurse thought she said Melody...that was made up?"

"Yes." Glory sniffled. "By your sister. She used to tease you with that silly story all the time. *We* never told you it was true."

Melody finally managed to lift her gaze. Her parents looked so vulnerable staring back at her. Their eyes were wide and expectant, like defendants waiting for a verdict. "Why didn't you tell me any of this before?"

The rest of the conversation played out like a made-for-TV movie about adoption. They'd wanted to tell her but could never find the right time. The love they felt for her was no different from their love for Candace. If they had to do it all over again, they wouldn't change a thing. They wouldn't stand in the way of helping her find her real parents, although the Achelous Agency closed one week after Melody was placed, so they wouldn't know where to begin....

How about with the fact that people have been doing whatever I ask them to? Or that the "trending" feathers in my hair have been landing on me all week? Or the possibility that I'm a RAD? Melody stood. Drained of her anger, she now felt only emptiness. What good were answers if they only led to more questions? "I need air."

"Sweetheart, you can't leave every time—"

"I'm not leaving. I mean, I am, but I'm fine," Melody said. And she meant it. "We're fine. I just feel like walking. I'll be home soon."

Her parents stood to hug her. This time she hugged back.

The night was disappointingly mild. An icy slap of wind might have sobered her sloshing thoughts but—

Omigod!

A woman was leaving Jackson's house.

They're back!

Melody dashed across Radcliffe Way. "Ms. J?" she whisper-called.

The woman sped up.

"Ms. J!" she called again, chasing the person down the dark street. "It's me, Melody."

The woman kept going.

"Stop!" Melody commanded. But unlike the others, the fleeing figure didn't obey. And before Melody could catch up, she was gone.

CHAPTER SIXTEEN
THE O.C.

If asked to describe the live recording of Lady Gaga's "Poker Face," Frankie would say *smoky and sullen, with bursts of giddiness*. The same way she'd describe her mood.

Gazing out the train window, playing and replaying the track on her iPhone, she also played and replayed her decision to meet up with Brett. What if her parents found out? What if it was a trap? What if Bekka was there with a hose full of makeup remover? What if Brett didn't show up? And what if he *did*? What if he proved his innocence and she fell for him all over again? Then what? A secret, long-distance RAD-normie relationship? That was the last thing she needed.

Clearly, no good could come of this. Frankie knew it the minute she agreed to the Saturday afternoon rendezvous. Still, curiosity had gotten the best of her. Not to mention she'd found the perfect tights and turtleneck for her plaid mini and was not above being admired, even by a heart-space breaker. Oh, and her hair—pulled high at the sides and clipped in the back—was va-va-va-voltage.

But wait. Billy. Mustn't forget about Billy. Abercrombie-hot, Six Flags–fun, hopelessly devoted, her fellow RAD was a mint catch—and her official date for the Gaga concert. *And* he didn't have a psycho-ex-girlfriend. Way better than Brett. But wait again. She had recently left D.J. for Brett. Now she was leaving Brett for Billy. What if she was a serial crusher? The type of girl in love with being in love? Like Drew Barrymore. Maybe Frankie wasn't capable of true feelings for anyone. In which case, she might as well love being in love with the RAD. So it was settled. Billy it was.

Frankie turned up the volume and listened to "Poker Face" again. Closing her eyes, she imagined the concert. Singing with Billy. Laughing as he got their entire row dancing. Feeling like a proud princess every time another girl checked him out. Her mother was right: Billy made more sense. The faster she cut ties with Brett, the sooner she could refocus her energy on liberating the RADs. With that, Frankie leaned back against the cream-colored seat and enjoyed the rest of her ride to Closuretown.

"Oregon City!" called the conductor.

The train slowed and then rolled to a stop. The station lacked the romance of, say, the Gare de Lyon in Paris, where art nouveau collides with Old World architecture. For one thing, there was no roof. No polished marble floors or flower vendors. No crying couples making the most of a final embrace. The station was a slab of concrete the same dreary color as the overcast sky.

Frankie stepped out onto the platform. The other passengers scattered like the Glitterati on cage-cleaning day. But she was totally unable to move. Smoky and sullen had morphed into scared and nervous. Bursts of giddiness were now sparks. Behind her, the doors kissed shut and the train continued north. There was no turning back.

"Welcome to the O.C.," called a familiar voice. Brett was waving from the last bench. The sight of his skull ring made Frankie's insides surge, dredging up what must have been the final crumbs of her feelings for him.

Rolling back her shoulders and swinging her amp purse, she strode toward him like a runway model.

"Can't read my,
Can't read my,
No, he can't read my poker face…"

Brett stood and hugged her. It felt awkward, strained by their collective insecurities.

"You look great."

"Thanks," she said, beaming. It would have been the time to tell him he looked great too, but up close Brett looked worn. His denim-blue eyes had faded. His spiky black hair hung limp. The black nail polish was gone. And his rugged outerwear had been replaced by a baggy maroon rain slicker. Still, Frankie felt a tug in her heart space. It was probably just one last crumb. Because like the 11:22 from Salem, that train had left the station.

154

"Ignore my clothes," he said, as if reading her mind. "They're my cousin's. I split town without packing."

Frankie nodded politely, still expecting a giant ambush. Instead, she got a box of assorted saltwater taffy.

"What's this?" she asked, knowing.

"I promised, didn't I?"

"Thanks." She smiled, resisting the urge to try a piece. *What if it's poisoned?* Instead, she sat. Screeching brakes on an incoming train provided a necessary distraction. They watched it pull away. "Listen, I think we should—" Frankie said at the exact same time Brett began speaking.

They giggled.

"You first," he said.

"No, you."

He swiveled to face her, then reached his arm across the back of the bench. His fingertips grazed her hair, warming her insides like a charge. "I can tell you still don't trust me. But I swear, I had nothing to do with the whole Channel Two thing. You have to believe me. I mean, look." He pulled the rain slicker away from his body. "Obviously, this has been rough on me too."

Has he always been this charming? She giggled and unwrapped a piece of strawberry taffy. The smell reminded her of Billy's Starburst.

"But the worst part is, I miss you, Stein." The lively flicker returned to his eyes.

He leaned forward.

She leaned back.

"Omigod, you would have loved what Melody did to Bekka in

155

bio the other day," Frankie blurted; she'd get to the cutting-ties part after she filled him in.

Brett smiled and gasped in all the right places. And then the flicker in his eyes started to dim. "So, did you really start hanging out with someone else?"

"Uh…" Frankie put the lid on the taffy box. Her sweet tooth was gone. She lowered her eyes and stared at the plaid pattern of her skirt until it blurred. Telling him about Billy would crush Brett. Not that there was anything to tell. They hadn't even kissed…*yet*. Still, she had made her choice. And it was a smart one. The right one.

"I'll be home as soon as those reporters forget about me. Probably in another day or two. Then things can go back to the way they were."

"No, they can't," Frankie said sadly.

He removed his arm from the back of the bench. Twirling his leather cuff, he asked, "Why?"

Frankie swallowed hard. "Brett, you know I think you're voltage, but everything is so dangerous right now, and with you being a normie and—"

"Maybe these will help change your mind." He dug into the crinkly pocket of the rain slicker and pulled out two tickets to the Lady Gaga concert.

Is this seriously happening?

"You're kidding, right?" she asked, more exasperated than excited. "How did you get those?"

"Ross from Channel Two," he said.

Frankie stiffened.

156

"*Be-fore* the show aired," he quickly added. "I was going to surprise you, but I think you've had enough surprises lately." He held out the tickets. "You in?"

A vision of Brett leaning over and kissing her during an acoustic set almost made Frankie accept. "Uh…" She began pulling the seams around her neck.

"Don't pick." Brett took her hand and lowered it. His touch Olympic-torched her insides. *Does he feel it too?* Frankie pulled her hand back. It felt like stepping away from a fireplace on a cold winter night.

"It's so nice of you to think of me and everything, but it would be better if we did our own thing for a while."

Brett was silent. Was he shocked? Sad? Angry? Frankie was too emotional to look.

"You should take 'em anyway," he said, placing the tickets in her hand. His touch torched her again. She couldn't meet his eyes.

"I can't." She stuffed them back into his pocket and stood.

"Frankie—"

She peered past his shoulder at the incoming train. Brakes screeched. It was time to go.

"It was good to see you again," she said, unsure if she should take the taffy or leave it. "If you want this back too, I understand—"

Before she knew what was happening, Brett was kissing her and she was kissing back. It felt like being showered in hot lava.

This wasn't a Paris train station. The floors weren't marble. And there wasn't a flower vendor for miles. Still, there they stood, a couple, close to crying, making the most of their final embrace.

CHAPTER SEVENTEEN
POWER FAILURE

Candace *click-clack*ed around her bedroom, putting the final touches on her date outfit. "I should have known you were adopted."

"What's that supposed to mean?" Melody asked.

"Going out on a Saturday night is not in your blood." She spritzed her Black Orchid perfume and then walked through its heady mist. "Now, will you step away from the window and stop spying on that house? You're acting like a sniper."

Letting the adoption jab slide, Melody released the powder-pink curtains and applauded her sister's proper use of *sniper*. But she was freaking out about Jackson. Ms. J had promised they would stay nearby, and yet Melody hadn't heard from him at all since they met at the coffee shop more than a week before. *Looks like it was good-bye after all.*

Meanwhile, Candace had been busting out *sister-from-another-mister* jokes all day—her way of dealing with shocking news. Melody had opted for the Jackson method—seek, accept, adapt. So far it was working perfectly. The truth had set her free. Now, if she could just find the strange woman who had run from his house…maybe she'd get some closure on Jackson's location too.

"How are these?" Candace asked.

Melody turned to find her glamour-loving sister wearing round, wire-frame glasses, a buttoned tweed blazer, and bootcut jeans. Her wild curls had been tamed into a bun, her feet jammed into sensible heels. "Ha! Maybe we are blood after all."

"Why? Do I look like a shut-in?" Candace turned to her full-length mirror and smoothed her blazer. " 'Cause I was going for a reader."

"Of *books*?"

"Yeah. Shane is a lit major at Willamette University, and for some reason he thinks I am too."

"Where did you meet him?" Melody asked, parting the curtains again and peering across the street.

"Freshman night at Corrigan's."

"Does he know you're a senior?"

"Yup."

"In *high school*?"

"Okay, sniper time is over," Candace said, dragging Melody out of her room. "Once I'm gone, feel free to crack open a bottle of Windex and have your way with my window. But now you have to leave."

"Why?" Melody asked, grabbing on to Candace's pewter bed-post.

Candace yanked her away. "Because Shane thinks I live alone." She shoved Melody into the hall and slammed the door.

"This is crazy, Can." Melody banged on the door. "I'm not going to hide just because you're living a double life. What's wrong with telling the truth every once in a while? It's not like you have a hard time getting a date."

"Stop shouting!" Candace called. "What if he hears you?"

"So what if he hears me? Maybe it's for the best. He's gonna find out eventua—"

"Omigod, Melly, the woman! She's back!"

Yes!

Melody dashed outside wearing striped J.Crew pajama bottoms and her black hoodie.

The cottage across the street was dark and lifeless. *Did she already go inside?*

Melody rang the bell.

"Sucka!" Candace called from her open window. "Call me Kevin, 'cause I am *Home Alone*!" She slapped her palms against her cheeks Macaulay Culkin–style, then slammed the window shut and closed her blinds.

Alone on Jackson's dark doorstep, Melody seethed. Hope hissed from her like an untied balloon. How could Candace toy with her like that? It was cruel beyond—

The door clicked open.

"Can I help you?" asked a woman, her voice clear and kind.

Startled, Melody whip-turned. There, in a pale seafoam-green jersey nightgown and matching robe—both the same color as her eyes—stood the elusive stranger.

Her quiet beauty was alluring. Messy black curls, skin like buttermilk, red lips dabbed with a hint of shine. Her figure was full, curvy, feminine—not fat. She was the type of woman artists longed to capture. And the type they never could.

"You're not sleepwalking, are you?" she asked, eyeing Melody's striped pajama bottoms and bare feet.

Melody shook her head and then peered into the dark house, hoping to discover something that could lead her to Jackson.

The woman closed the door until there was just enough space for her head to poke through. "I'm sorry, what's your name?"

"Melody." She paused so the stranger could introduce herself, but the woman never did. "I, um, I'm friends with the owner. Well, really more with her son, Jackson, and I haven't seen him for a while, so I came to check in. You know, to make sure they're okay."

The stranger offered nothing but the same warm smile.

"So, do, um, do you know if they're okay?"

She shook her head. "I'm just renting the house."

"For how long?"

"Month to month."

"Do you know where they went?" Melody tried.

"Nope." The woman shrugged. "All I know is they're going somewhere next Saturday by private jet," she offered. "It sounded fancy."

Melody's heart free-fell into her stomach. Was Jackson really leaving this time? And if so, why wasn't he trying to say good-bye? Her persuasive voice had convinced Ms. J to stay the first time; all she had to do was find Jackson's mom and convince her again. But what if Melody's power was deteriorating? That would explain why this woman hadn't stopped running the other night when Melody called to her. Unless, of course, she was too far out of range. Or it was an eye-contact thing, or maybe the wind diluted its strength, or...

Melody stamped her foot in frustration. She didn't know what was happening to her, and she had zero clue whom to ask. She didn't know who her birth mother was! She didn't know where Jackson was! She didn't know how to get him back! She didn't know anything!

"Are you okay?"

"No," Melody said, surprised by her own honesty. But this stranger was the only lead she had, and she was going to make the most of it. All she had to do was look the woman in the eye, speak clearly, and ask. "Do you know where Jackson is?"

Melody waited for the blinking. It never came. "I don't. I'm sorry."

"What about a boy named D.J.? Have you ever met him?"

"No."

Without the blinking, it was hard to gauge whether the stranger was telling the truth. Knowing that liars need time to think, Melody served up questions like high-speed Ping-Pong. "Where are you sending the rent checks?"

"To a post office box here in Salem."

"Why are you renting their house?"

"I need a place to live."

The faster Melody asked, the faster the woman answered.

"Where did you meet the owner?"

"I didn't. I got the house through a real estate agent."

"Why is it so dark in there?"

"I'm...well, I guess you could say I'm green."

Score! A RAD! Like Frankie!

"Omigod, I can help you. I'm actually the same as you. Kind of. I'm not green, but I have other attributes. I think..." Melody realized she was rambling, and giggled. "Sorry. I'm just excited. Look, you don't have to be scared anymore. Just let me inside, and we'll—"

"Excuse me?"

"Can we just go inside?"

"I'm sorry, but no," she said, closing the door even more.

"Listen, I'm on your side, okay?" Melody insisted. "I'm a lot more like you than you know."

The woman smiled a distant smile, nostalgic and a bit reserved. "And how's that?"

"I have something to hide too." Melody paused, silently urging herself to hold back. But there was something about this woman that made her feel safe. And everything about her secret felt too heavy to carry alone. "I can use my voice to persuade people to do things," she blurted. It was the first time Melody had said those words aloud. They sounded even more insane than they did when she was thinking them. But a green woman was in no position to judge.

Opening the door just enough to reveal herself but not the house, the woman sighed. "Sounds dangerous."

Melody raised her eyebrows. Was this woman mocking her? "*Dangerous*? What do you mean by that?"

"I mean"—she gripped the gold sailboat charm on her necklace and dragged it back and forth on the chain—"that people need to be free to make their own decisions."

"What if their decisions are bad ones?" Melody asked. Like *the school board's firing of Ms. J.*

"Who are you to decide that?"

Melody's chest tightened. "I know the difference between right and wrong."

The woman refastened her robe and folded her arms across her chest. "Just because something is right for you doesn't mean it's right for everyone."

Who does this woman think she is, anyway? "Well, in this case it is."

The woman narrowed her seafoam-green eyes. "What case?"

"The person you're renting this house from was fired because of discrimination, and now she's leaving in a week and—" Suddenly, Melody's breath caught on something sharp: a solution. "Omigod, I could just tell Principal Weeks to give Ms. J her job back! I could tell everyone at school to welcome her back and—"

"Stop," the woman ordered, her voice firm but still kind. "You can't do that."

"Why?" Melody asked indignantly, again stamping her bare foot on the pavement like a child.

"Because that would change the course of events and alter her destiny," the woman insisted.

"Yeah. For the better!"

"It's wrong, Melody. And it's dangerous."

"Well, what good is this power if I can't use it?"

"No one said it was good. In fact, it sounds terrible. Find

another way to get her job back. A way that doesn't involve your...*attribute*. A way that just involves you."

"Ha!" Melody said, nowhere close to laughing. "It's kind of hard to take *be yourself* advice from someone who's ashamed of her skin color."

"Ashamed? I'm not ashamed of my skin color."

"Oh, really," Melody said. "Well, if you like being green so much, why are you living in the dark?"

The woman backed into the house and giggled. "To save electricity," she said, as if it should have been obvious. "It's one of the many steps I've taken to live a more environmentally conscious life."

Oh. That kind of green.

Humiliation zip-lined from Melody's head to her toes. How could she have been so stupid? So trusting? So desperate? *What if this normie was a RAD-hater? What if she called the police?* "Um, I'd better go."

"Wait." The woman rested her warm hand on Melody's shoulder. "If you really care about this Jackson boy, you'll let things unfold the way they were meant to. Not the way you want them to." The conviction in her eyes could not be ignored. This woman obviously felt strongly about her message.

But why? She was just a tree-hugging normie who probably thought Melody had made everything up. Still, she wouldn't release her grip until she heard what she wanted. "Promise me you'll try."

"Okay," Melody said. "I'll *try*."

Satisfied, the woman smiled and then closed the door, leaving Melody alone and in the dark once again.

CHAPTER EIGHTEEN
A WHIRLWIND BROMANCE

It was that time of the month.

Clawdeen didn't have to look up to know the moon was almost full. She could feel it. Every time Lala urged her to "brake" or "turn the wheel," she wanted to cry, rip her friend's tongue out, or both.

"Why don't we skip the parallel stuff and try regular parking?" Lala said, eyeing the empty lot in front of the inn. Her pallor was no longer caused by hunger or lack of sunlight (thanks to Harriet's cooking and Lala's daily hikes with Clawd) but rather by Clawdeen's jerky driving.

"What's the point?" Clawdeen pouted. "I'll never get my license."

"Anything's possible," Lala said. "Watch." She popped off the cap of her matte red lipstick and swiped it across her mouth with newfound confidence. "Not a single smear on my cheek."

"How'd you do that?" Clawdeen asked, knowing how hard it

was for the vamp, who couldn't see her reflection, to color inside the lines.

"I can do my eyes too." Lala smiled, batting her smudge-free mascaraed lashes.

"Did you learn that in Romania?" Clawdeen asked, casually turning down the heat.

Lala leaned forward and turned it back up. "No, today. While you were napping. Clawd helped me."

"Clawd?" *Again?*

First he persuaded Lala to taste steak. Granted, she fang-speared it and then spit it into a napkin, but still. It was the closest she'd ever come to a real bite. Then he got her to embrace natural light (and a lack of sleep) on their parasol-free sunrise hikes. Now *this*?

"Yeah." Lala giggled at the memory. "He made a papier-mâché mold of my face, and we practiced on that."

"That hairy, football-playing meathead helped you put on *makeup*?" Clawdeen asked, knowing Clawd was a much better catch than the oaf she'd just described. But the guy who arts-and-crafted a mask to teach Lala how to apply MAC was not the Clawd she knew. The Clawd she knew cared about yard lines, not lip lines; blitzes, not blushes; formations, not foundations. Maybe he was feeling the effects of the waxing moon? The stress of life in hiding? Or ball withdrawal.

Lala rubbed her fangs to check for lipstick. For the first time in the history of their friendship, her index finger came back clean. "Well, he won't be hairy for long."

"What's *that* supposed to mean?" Clawdeen asked, hearing

the possessiveness in her own voice. But who was she possessive of? Her brother? Her best friend? Or the way she used to be the first to know?

"It means we made a deal," Lala said, wrapping her black cashmere scarf around her slight shoulders. "He said if I mastered my makeup, he'd let me give him a mohawk."

"Fur real?"

"Yup, as soon as your driving lesson is done. Signed a contract and everything." She pulled a piece of paper from her skinny-jeans pocket and flashed Clawd's signature.

"Shut the duck up!" Clawdeen stomped on the pedal under her foot. The truck lunged forward. "Ahhhhhh!"

"Stop!" Lala screamed as they careered toward a metal Dumpster by the side of the inn.

Clawdeen jammed on the brakes with the force of someone who just realized her older brother had a crush on her best friend. The scrappy jock who liked peppy blonds and the serious brunette who insisted on a gentleman? *Really?* And then, *SLAP!* The air bags inflated.

Everything became silent.

"I think that's enough for today," Lala mumbled, her perfectly painted lips pressed against the puffy cushion. "Wanna come watch the haircut?"

Clawdeen shook her head. She felt snippy enough.

Instead, she opted to keep her face hidden inside the cornstarch-scented pouf until life made sense again.

TO: Clawdeen
oct 27, 9:22 PM
CLEO: TENT LOOKS GOLDEN. CAN'T BELIEVE UR STILL HAVING THE SASSY. EVERYONE ASSUMED IT WAS CANCELED. ^^^^

TO: Cleo
oct 27, 9:22 PM
CLAWDEEN: HUH? #####

TO: Clawdeen
oct 27, 9:23 PM
CLEO: THE TENT IN YOUR FRONT YARD. LOVE IT! ^^^^

TO: Cleo
oct 27, 9:23 PM
CLAWDEEN: FUR REAL? ####

TO: Cleo
oct 27, 9:24 PM
CLAWDEEN: OMG! MY PARENTS FORGOT TO CANCEL EVERYTHING. ####

TO: Cleo
oct 27, 9:24 PM
CLAWDEEN: THE SASSY CAN STILL HAPPEN!!!! ####

TO: Clawdeen

oct 27, 9:24 PM

CLEO: THANK GEB I DIDN'T RETURN MY DRESS. I CAN'T WAIT TO SEND DEUCE PICTURES OF ME MAKING OUT WITH EVERY GUY ON THE BBALL TEAM. ^^^^

TO: Cleo

oct 27, 9:24 PM

CLAWDEEN: STILL HAVEN'T HEARD FROM HIM? ####

TO: Clawdeen

oct 27, 9:24 PM

CLEO: DON'T WANT TO TALK ABOUT IT. WHAT ABOUT UR PARENTS? U GONNA CRY UNTIL THEY CHANGE THEIR MINDS? ^^^^

TO: Cleo

oct 27, 9:25 PM

CLAWDEEN: NOT GONNA TELL THEM. SHHH! ☺ ####

TO: Clawdeen

oct 27, 9:25 PM

CLEO: I LOVE A GOOD DECEPTION PLOT. HOW CAN I HELP? ^^^^

TO: Cleo

oct 27, 9:25 PM

CLAWDEEN: MAKE SURE EVERYONE GOES. ####

TO: Clawdeen
oct 27, 9:25 PM
CLEO: MIGHT BE A BETTER JOB FOR MELODY. SHE'S BEEN ROYALLY PERSUASIVE. DON'T WORRY, I'M STILL MORE POPULAR THOUGH. ☺ ^^^^

TO: Cleo
oct 27, 9:25 PM
CLAWDEEN: CAN U WORK ON DECORATIONS? IF I DO MY PARENTS WILL SUSPECT. ####

TO: Clawdeen
oct 27, 9:25 PM
CLEO: SURE. I'LL GET BEB AND HASINA ON IT ASAP. HOW R U GOING TO GET HERE? NOT GONNA RUN THROUGH THE WOODS, R U? YOU'LL BE ALL SWEATY. ^^^^

TO: Cleo
oct 27, 9:25 PM
CLAWDEEN: HOPING LALA CAN DRIVE ME. IF SHE'S NOT TOO BUSY WITH HER NEW BF. ####

TO: Clawdeen
oct 27, 9:27 PM
CLEO: HUH? WHAT BF? ^^^^

TO: Melody
oct 27, 9:28 PM
CLAWDEEN: GONNA HAVE MY SASSY. NOT TELLING PARENTS. CLEO SAID YOU COULD GET EVERYONE TO GO. CAN U? ####

TO: Clawdeen
oct 27, 9:34 PM
MELODY: NO PROB.

TO: Melody
oct 27, 9:34 PM
CLAWDEEN: THX. I OWE U! ####

TO: Clawdeen
oct 27, 9:39 PM
CLEO: CAT GOT UR THUMB? U STILL THERE? WHAT BOYFRIEND? ^^^^

TO: Cleo
oct 27, 9:39 PM
CLAWDEEN: SORRY. G2G GET OUT OF THIS AIR BAG AND CHECK CLAWD'S NEW MOHAWK. KEEP ME POSTED. SEE U AT THE SASSY…SOMEHOW. ####

TO: Clawdeen
oct 27, 9:40 PM
CLEO: AIR BAG? MOHAWK? WHAT MOHAWK? WHAT'S HAPPENING OVER THERE? ^^^^

TO: Clawdeen
oct 27, 9:42 PM
CLEO: KA! FORGET U. GONNA TRY LALA. ^^^^

CHAPTER NINETEEN
JOE KSONYOU

This lunchtime playlist is mocking me, Melody thought as she and Candace raced around the cafeteria on Friday afternoon gathering signatures to the tune of Britney Spears's "Till the World Ends."

If only she had marched into Principal Weeks's office on Monday morning, like she wanted to, and demanded he give Ms. J her job back. Maybe then Jackson's mom would be teaching bio this afternoon. And if Melody had told every normie in town to accept the RADs and welcome them back to Salem, maybe Jackson would be with her right now. But she hadn't. Instead, she'd let some stranger with seafoam-green eyes persuade her to get them back the normie way. To avoid altering destiny and changing the course of events forever. Ha! Like the current course was something worth clinging to.

Still, Melody had promised not to use her powers of persuasion on Principal Weeks, and she intended to keep that promise. So she used Candace's.

Unfortunately, the Monday morning meeting hadn't gone the way she hoped. Rather than caving in to the blond, as most guys did, Principal Weeks stood his ground. He explained that the decision to let Ms. J go had been made by the board, not him. Appealing was an option, but only if they drafted a letter asking to reinstate the teacher and got it signed by one hundred students. If he had it for his weekly Friday conference with the board, he'd present it. If not...well, that didn't matter. If not, Ms. J and Jackson would be en route to who-knows-where the following night, and Melody would hunt down the woman with the seafoam-green eyes, flick on all her lights, and make her *pay*.

Ping!

Melody stopped in the middle of the buzzy cafeteria and checked her phone.

to: **Melody**

oct 29, 12:33 PM

CLAWDEEN: HAVE YOU TOLD EVERYONE THE SASSY IS STILL ON? ####

Oops. She had completely forgotten to spread the word. But she would, the minute her petition was complete.

to: **Clawdeen**

oct 29, 12:34 PM

MELODY: YUP. IT'S GOING TO BE PACKED.

174

Candace clicked her pen. "Come on, Melly. We only need six more."

"You've asked everyone in here," Melody said, somehow managing to take her sister seriously in what had become Candace's "NUDI duty" uniform: a beige trench coat, stilettos, artfully spray-tanned legs, and her "reading" glasses. She was convinced the *sexy-flasher-meets-university-lit-major* look conveyed both NUDI and duty. Which it did...when her audience was male. Females, however, were less responsive. It took all of Melody's control not to grab the clipboard and force everyone to sign. But she had made a promise.

It was 12:38. There were seven minutes left until the bell *bwoop*ed. "Maybe we should try the bathrooms," Melody suggested.

"Ew, no." Candace shuddered. "The lunch special was bean burritos. There's got to be someone we missed." She scanned the zoned-off cafeteria and began muttering. "Peanut-Free for RADs—got 'em. Gluten-Free for RADs—yup. Lactose-Free for RADs—check. The Fat-Frees were anti-RAD, and we hit up every guy in the Allergy-Free Zone." She tapped her pen against the clipboard.

The music on the playlist began to mellow, an indication that lunch period was winding down. Soda cans were being crunched, milk cartons stomped on. All around them, students were taking their final bites as Alicia Keys appropriately sang "No One."

"Maybe if you were wearing clothes, the girls would sign," Melody snapped, feeling the pressure.

"What are you talking about? I got Frankie Stein, Cleo de Nile, Julia Phelps, Abbey Bominable, Spectra Vondergeist—"

"I mean *normie* girls," Melody hissed. "What about them?" Six wannabe fashion-forward ninth graders were busing their trays.

"They already said no," Candace insisted.

"Try again," Melody insisted back, cheating just a little.

Candace blinked rapidly. "'Scuse me," she said to the group. "I'm sure you already know that biology teacher Ms. J has been—"

"Look!" said the brunette with shoulder-length waves and green glitter shadow. Instead of eyeing Candace's provocative "uniform," she was pointing at Melody. "Cute feathers!" Then to her friend she gushed, "Mandie, see how they stay in her hair? We need *that* kind. The ones you bought at Michaels were like scraps from a stripper boa."

The others nodded in agreement.

"Maybe next time *you* should go," Mandie mumbled under her breath.

Her so-called friends exchanged quick eye rolls.

"'Scuse me." The blond with a side braid and a plaid fedora tugged the sleeve of Melody's striped sweater. "Would you ever in a million years tell us where you got those feathers? We won't post it."

Melody smiled. "They kinda just fell from the sky." *Now will you please just sign!*

"I told you she wouldn't tell us," said the pink-streaked pixie.

"They came from the endangered Carver bird," Candace announced. "The species sheds once every four years over a remote bear cave in Montana. Melody here, a celebrated bird-watcher, is the only one who knows the cave's exact location." Candace probably assumed the feathers came from the ravine, but she had been so proud of her sister's signature look that she'd been promoting it like a pop-up shop.

The freshmen gawked at Melody with renewed interest, their expressions a mix of wonder and geek-pity.

Candace checked her surroundings and then summoned them closer. In a gossip-sharing whisper she said, "Did you know that"—she glanced over her shoulder—"Christian Dior hired Melody to gather Carver feathers for his spring collection?"

They shook their heads.

"You obviously haven't seen his couture dresses," Candace said, her tone seasoned with a dash of snob and a dollop of *shame-on-you*.

Melody's cheeks burned as the girls eyed her with newfound respect. Her sister was obviously working an angle. But which one?

"Christian offered fifty thousand euros to get his hands on ten more. Turns out Taylor Swift wanted to wear them in her updo at the Emmys. But Melly said she gave him everything." Candace winked conspiratorially. "Shh. What happens at a bear cave in Montana stays at a bear cave in Montana. *Right?*"

Tickled to be in on the secret, the girls giggle-nodded.

"But," Candace bellowed, adjusting her glasses, "if you sign our petition and *promise* not to tell Christian, you can each have one."

She peeked at Melody to see if that was okay. Melody nodded. She had an entire drawerful of them at home.

Squealing with delight, the girls took turns scribbling their names in the last six spaces on the sheet. After each signature, Melody pulled an olive and blue feather from her hair and handed it over. "Careful with the tip," she added. "It's real gold."

Candace held in a laugh.

"We promise," they said, almost in unison. After ditching their trays on the nearest table, they hurried off to spend some much-needed time with their locker mirrors.

"Done!" Melody high-fived her sister, her pride double what it would have been had she used her persuasive power.

Candace jammed the pen into her ballerina bun and declared, "Mrs. Stern-Figgus out!" Then, like a superhero exhibitionist, she untied her trench and let it fall to the sticky floor, revealing a prim pink blouse with a flouncy neck bow and Hudsons cuffed to her thighs. She unrolled the jeans, kicked off her heels, pulled a pair of flats from her back pocket, and scooped up her coat. "To the principal's office!"

Melody burst out laughing, wondering if she would be confident and free-spirited like Candace if they shared the same blood. Not that it really mattered: They shared a life. And for that she was grateful.

Candace and Melody charged past the buxom secretary toward the half-open door of Principal Weeks's office.

"Ladies!" called Mrs. Saunders, pulling off her headset. "Fifth period has started—"

"It's okay," Candace insisted. "We have a note."

"It doesn't matter." The secretary stood. "He's in a meeting."

"Ignore us," Melody insisted.

Mrs. Saunders began blinking and then sat. "Will do."

"Dang, we make a good team," Candace said, tossing her coat onto an empty chair.

Melody eyed the clipboard in her sister's hand. They really did work well together.

"Sir?" Candace knocked, and then pulled Melody into the principal's office. It smelled like meatballs and cologne.

Principal Weeks quickly closed out a window on his computer and sat up straighter. "Shouldn't you be in class?"

"Absolutely," Candace said, with more sugar than Frosted Flakes. "We just wanted to give you this." She approached his desk with such confidence that her blouse bow bounced.

"And it is...?" He wrapped his half-eaten sandwich in waxed paper and pushed it aside.

"The petition for your board meeting today," Melody said.

He narrowed his eyes in confusion.

"To get Ms. J back," she added.

"Ah, yes," he said, remembering. "If I recall, I said I needed one hundred signatures to—"

Candace waved the clipboard. "Got 'em."

"You found one hundred Merston students to stand up for *Ms. J*?"

Candace nodded proudly.

"Not *everyone* is afraid of RADs, you know," Melody said.

"True, but I hear her pop quizzes are terrifying." He burst out laughing.

"Sir." Melody clenched her fists. "You need to take this seriously."

Candace turned around and hissed, "Melly!"

It's okay, she mouthed back.

Principal Weeks began blinking. "You're right."

"Maybe some of the parents are afraid of change, but the students are not. We want it. And we're not afraid to say it," Melody went on.

"Prejudice out!" Candace said, handing him the clipboard.

"People couldn't wait to sign," Melody added for effect.

"Is that so?" said Principal Weeks, scanning the signatures.

The girls nodded confidently.

Snickering, he asked, "Then how do you explain this?" He offered the clipboard to Candace and folded his arms across his wrinkled gray suit. Reading over her sister's orchid-scented shoulders, Melody gasped. There were one hundred names on the petition, but only a dozen were real. The others read like the corny *Jokes for the John* bathroom book her father had gotten at an office holiday party.

Ima Horny...Emma Loser...Sue Age...N.M.E. Agent... Ray D. Aider...Mort U. Airy...Terri Aki...Colin Allcars... Dennis Anyone...Hal Apenyo...Jerry Atric...Tony Award... Oscar Goesto...May Balleen...Fallon Doun...Kent Gedup...

Melody couldn't go on. Tears began to form, pinching the backs of her eyes. The names began to blur. Dizzy from a cyclone of humiliation and defeat, she tried to focus on the maples outside the window. But their leafless branches made her feel more alone.

"Didn't you check them?" she whispered to her sister.

Candace sighed. "Maybe they were too afraid to give their real names."

"Sorry, girls," Principal Weeks said sincerely. "I know how hard you tried. And between us, I wish things would change around here too. But I have a board to please and..."

Melody wanted to cover her ears and scream. Why were adults so afraid of taking a stand? Could a job really be more valuable than human decency? Progress more terrifying than stagnation? Coexistence more threatening than war? Melody hated herself for listening to that woman. So what if she changed the course of events? Wasn't that the point?

"Principal Weeks," she said, interrupting his butt-kissing ode to the board. Maybe he was scared to use his voice, but Melody wasn't. Not anymore. "I insist that you—"

Beep.

Mrs. Saunders's voice crackled over the intercom. "Caroline Madden on line one for you, sir."

"Excuse me," he said, stiffening. "I have to take this call, girls."

"But—"

"Hang in there," he said, and then picked up the phone. "Caroline, hi. How's Bekka feeling?"

Candace, who had no experience with rejection, snapped, "NUDIs out!" and slammed the principal's door behind them. She grabbed her coat, mumbled something about not being able to wait for college, and then ditched school for the rest of the day.

Melody, however, had no intention of sulking. She promised that woman she'd *try* not to use her powers, and she had tried. And failed. This time she would do things her way.

For the rest of the afternoon, she told every RAD-hater she could find to go to Clawdeen's Sassy Sixteen. Once they'd gathered, she would order them to embrace all RADs and unite them on a mission to bring back Ms. J from wherever she was planning to go.

Jackson would come home.

The controlling environmentalist with the seafoam-green eyes would leave.

Clawdeen's party would go down as the event that brought everyone together.

And destiny would be changed forever.

Finally.

TO: Cleo

oct 30, 1:07 PM

CLAWDEEN: COUNTDOWN BEGINS. SASSY 7 HOURS AWAY. HOW R THE DECORATIONS? ####

TO: Clawdeen

oct 30, 1:07 PM

CLEO: BEB AND HASINA HAVE BEEN WORKING ON THEM ALL MORNING. THEY'RE OVER THERE SETTING UP NOW. GONNA TEXT ME WHEN THEY'RE DONE SO I CAN DO A FINAL WALK-THROUGH. I'LL SEND PICS. DANCE FLOOR IS DOWN, DJ BOOTH CAME. JUST WAITING FOR CATERER. ^^^^

TO: Cleo

oct 30, 1:08 PM

CLAWDEEN: OMG, TOTALLY SPACED! MOM WAS GOING TO DO THE CATERING. WE HAVE NO FOOD!!! ####

TO: Clawdeen

oct 30, 1:10 PM

CLEO: I'LL PUT BEB AND HASINA ON IT WHEN THEY FINISH DECORATING. ALL YOU HAVE TO WORRY ABOUT IS SNEAKING OUT, LOOKING GOLDEN, AND NOT GETTING CAUGHT. BTW, PREPARE YOUR EARS FOR A TRIP 2 EMERALD CITY! AUNT NEFERTITI'S ANGELINA JOLIE EARRINGS WILL BE WAITING FOR YOU WHEN U ARRIVE. HAPPY BIRTHDAY! ^^^^

TO: Cleo
oct 30, 1:11 PM
CLAWDEEN: FUR REAL? OMG, THX. WHERE WOULD I BE WITHOUT U? ####

TO: Clawdeen
oct 30, 1:11 PM
CLEO: THE HIDEOUT INN. ☺ G2G GET GORGEOUS. I HAVE A BBALL TEAM TO CORRUPT. TTYL ^^^^

TO: Melody
oct 30, 1:13 PM
CLAWDEEN: IS EVERYONE COMING? ####

TO: Clawdeen
oct 30, 1:13 PM
MELODY: SOME HAVE LADY GAGA TIX, SO THEY'LL BE LATE. EVERYONE ELSE SAID YES.

TO: Melody
oct 30, 1:14 PM
CLAWDEEN: YAY! BUMMED ABOUT THE RADS WHO AREN'T HERE. ####

TO: Clawdeen
oct 30, 1:14 PM
MELODY: ME 2. ☺ GOOD LUCK SNEAKING OUT. HAPPY BIRTHDAY SASSY. SEE U L8R.

CHAPTER TWENTY

MOTHER TRUCKER

Clawdeen's phone *ping*ed with another *what's your ETA?* text from Cleo, and she quickly shut it off.

"Remind me why I planned my Sassy Sixteen so close to the full moon?" she asked Lala as they descended the inn's green-carpet staircase.

"We all warned you," she insisted, wagging her pale finger. "But you insisted it had to be date-accurate or it would feel fake."

"Well, I wish you'd made me un-insist. So far I've spent my entire birthday waxing, clipping my nails, and peeing."

"Whaddaya think would happen after you drank two pots of that Tame and Tranquil herbal tea?" She smiled, her newly White-stripped fangs proudly on display.

"I had to do *something*," Clawdeen snapped. "I transition in two days. I'm having severe mood-management issues." She stopped to check her curls in the foyer mirror. Still full and shiny, they had at least three more hours before new growth dragged down their bounce. Plenty of time to make an entrance and pose for pictures.

"Maybe it's a good thing the Sassy was canceled," Lala said, standing beside Clawdeen and reglossing her gloss. After years of friendship, Clawdeen was still caught off guard by the vamp's missing reflection. "Now you don't have to worry about accidentally eating anyone."

"La!"

"I'm *kidding*." Lala giggled. "Anyway, celebrating with your family will be fun."

Clawdeen nodded, anxious for the moment when she could fill her friend in on the plan. Withholding the truth from Lala felt like repressing a giant cherry Coke burp. But they still had the family dinner to get through. If Cleo's relationship with Deuce had taught her anything, it was that crushes and secret-keeping didn't mix. All that making out must loosen the jaw joints, allowing classified information to escape. One slipup by Lala, and Clawdeen's special night would be more busted than a perp on *Law & Order*. No amount of burp relief was worth that.

Once in the lobby, Lala teetered toward the restaurant in her gray open-toed booties so she could get the door for Clawdeen. Her silky high ponytail wagging with glee, the vamp looked fetching in a dark plum chiffon ruffle minidress. Her skin had a kiss of color, her makeup application was flawless, and her wise black eyes seemed lit from within. Ever since she arrived, her style had become less Jenni and more Woww. At least tonight her hotness wouldn't be wasted on the transitioning Wolf brothers. It would be whisked away to an unforgettable party and admired by Merston High's elite. Clawdeen couldn't wait for Lala to find out. She was going to freak.

"Hungry?" Lala asked her friend sheepishly.

"Not really," answered Clawdeen, even though her appetite had been raging all day. Despite her mounting desire to feast, she'd managed to quell her instincts with endless gum chewing, like a true Hollywood party girl. After all, she had a size-four dress to squeeze into and a dance floor to dominate. Disco balls tonight. Meatballs tomorrow.

"Well, that's too bad because..." Lala pushed open the doors and shouted, "Surprise!"

What the...?

Pink's "Raise Your Glass" began blaring from the speakers. In time with the chorus, Don stood and raised a carton of milk. "We know how badly you wanted a Sassy Sixteen, so here it is." As usual, the serving dishes were half empty, her brothers' bellies already half full.

"Forks down," Lala insisted, not realizing how much willpower that required at this time of the month. Yet somehow, whether out of love for their sister or lust for her best friend, the boys managed. On her three-count, they began singing "Happy Birthday" on bended knee.

When they were through, Clawdeen applauded wildly. Eyes welling with tears, she thank-hugged them all while Harriet snapped pictures. "This is insane," she said, admiring their efforts.

HAPPY SASSY SIXTEEN, DEENIE! had been spray-painted across a gigantic banner made of old white tablecloths that stretched from the bar all the way to the fireplace mantel. The tables were covered in lit votives that cast frolicking shadows on the stone walls. The seats—filled by the salvaged mannequins from her father's construction job—were lifting champagne flutes of what Clawdeen assumed to be sparkling cider. Thanks to a scanner, old yearbooks, and a photo printer with the zoom feature, each mannequin wore the face of someone on her Sassy guest list. The gesture reminded Clawdeen of Perez Hilton—creepy and awesome at the same time.

Her heart swelled with emotion. In spite of their chauvinistic old-school values, she adored her brothers. They obviously adored her too. If they only knew she planned to flee the instant the smoke cleared on her candles. She felt guilty just thinking about it.

"Dad is so sorry he couldn't be here," her mother said, popping the lens cap on her Nikon.

"It's okay," Clawdeen replied, meaning it. Escaping would be way easier without her father sniffing around.

"He tried to get away for the night," Harriet continued, "but the Panisses are huge clients...."

Nino burst out laughing. "She said huge Paniss."

The boys cracked up. Clawdeen did too. Lala shivered.

Clawd took off his navy cardigan and draped it over her shoulders. Lala acted surprised by his gesture. He shrugged, like he would have done it for anyone. Like celebrities on a movie set, they kidded themselves into thinking their relationship was a secret. As if maintaining his precious mohawk wasn't a big enough indicator of how devoted he was to her already.

"Wait," Harriet said, beaming. "You have to open your present."

Rocks reached under the table and presented Clawdeen with a Singer XL-150. "It's a karaoke machine," he announced.

"No, it's not," Howie said, whacking Rocks on the head with his napkin. "It's a sewing machine."

"Oh, okay." Rocks rolled his eyes. "That's why it says Singer, genius."

They laughed.

Clawdeen searched her mother's caramel-colored eyes, wondering how the family could afford something so high-tech.

"It was Nino's idea, but we all pitched in," she said, sensing her daughter's concern. "Suite nine needs some new bedding, and I was hoping you could make it."

Clawdeen's heart thumped against her rib cage. "Nino!"

He covered his face with a napkin. "Sorry," he muttered. "I didn't want to stand there filming while you sewed it all by hand. It would have taken hours."

"It was either that or wrap up Mr. Stein," Don joked.

Everyone laughed, except Clawdeen. Thanks to her brother's betrayal, she was about to end up like a Colombian coffee bean—grounded for life.

"Don't worry, Mom. I'll take it all down. I promise."

"Why? It looks great." Harriet smiled. "Now that you're sixteen, you should have your own bathroom, so it's all yours."

Clawdeen jumped up and hug-thanked her mother twice: once for giving her life and a second time for letting her decorate it. Creative license today, driver's license tomorrow! She had finally tasted her first slice of freedom pie. But instead of feeling satisfied, Clawdeen craved more. It was that sweet.

After all of them stuffed themselves with Harriet's decadent seven-layer chocolate cake, the guys hurried off to watch football. Lala planned to meet Clawd by the fireplace after the game so she could "kick his hairy behind in checkers." But Clawdeen asked if they could schedule their match for another night. It was her birthday, and she wanted some girl time. *Alone.* Lala flicked herself in the fangs for being so dense and was more than happy to oblige.

"Wanna make some curtains for our new room?" Clawdeen asked, faking conversation until they were out of earshot. Harriet, who was closing down the dining room, had the best hearing in the family. So it was always wise to err on the side of caution.

"Did your dad really get all those mannequins from a construction job?" Lala asked.

"Yup. He tore down an old department store and kept them. You should see what he brings home from jobs. I have an entire shed full of junk. Tires, fabric, nails, cell-phone batteries..."

"Really." Lala yawned. "Sounds exciting."

"Oh, it is. You really should see it sometime."

When they finally reached the lobby, Clawdeen gripped Lala's cold hand and pulled her down the hall. "What are you—?"

"Shhh!"

"Oh," Lala whispered, finally catching on.

With a silencing finger to her lips, Clawdeen led her friend into the ladies' room and blasted the water over the sound of piped-in jazz music. The double-stalled safe haven, stocked with satchels of potpourri, rose-colored bulbs, fuzzy toilet-seat covers, woven area rugs, peach curtains, and two-ply tissue, stood in stark contrast to the manly-man decor of the inn.

Clawdeen reached under the basin's pink pleated skirt. She pulled out matching L.L.Bean totes, a garment bag, and keys to the maintenance truck. "Let's get sassy!"

Lala gripped her stomach. "Can we take a break on the driving lessons?" she asked. "I ate a ton and—"

"*You're* driving, not me," Clawdeen explained, wiggling out of her jeans.

"Where are we going?" Lala asked, twirling her high pony.

"My party," Clawdeen said, as if it should have been obvious. "It's on!"

"How?"

"Cleo's been helping with the setup, and Melody's been in charge of the guest list. It's gonna be packed."

"Fang-*tastic*!" Lala said, beaming, and then asked, "Wait, why did Melody know about it before I did?"

"My parents have no clue. We're sneaking out." Clawdeen unzipped her green wool hoodie and tossed it onto the rug. "I made a dress for you, but what you're wearing is perfect. Plum is such a peachy color on you."

Lala turned away and pinkie-dabbed gloss on her lips.

"I still can't believe you can do that without smearing it all over your face." Clawdeen smiled. She was too excited to feel slighted by Lala's recent bond with Clawd. Besides, there was a time and place for petty emotions. The time was sooo yesterday, and the place was middle school. Anyone with her own bedroom and a Singer XL-150 was far too mature for such grievances—or should at least pretend to be.

"Well?" Lala said, folding her pale arms across her chest.

"Well, *what*?"

"Well, why didn't you tell me?" she pressed.

Clawdeen kicked off her flats. "I didn't want my mom to find out."

"Seriously?" Lala pushed back the sleeves of Clawd's cardigan. "Why would I tell your *mom*?"

"You wouldn't. You'd tell my brother, and *he*'d tell my mom."

"He doesn't *know*?"

"Of course not," Clawdeen snapped, irked by Lala's irk. They were supposed to be speed-prepping and giggle-snorting, dizzy with the excitement and danger of it all. Doing each other's hair and zipping each other's dresses. Holding hands and running through the parking lot, wobbling in their heels and fumbling with the car keys. Blasting their iPods. Planning Clawdeen's entrance... anything but *this*.

"So Clawd's not going?"

"No, he's not going. None of them are." Clawdeen opened her garment bag and blew a kiss at the lilac-gray masterpiece inside. The deep V, the iridescent sheen, the metallic black sash... "Can I knock off a Diane von Furstenberg wrap dress or what?" If only she had time to slip into it with grace. Instead, she threw it on like a frenzied runway model during Fashion Week and hurried into her snakeskin booties. Moon-shmoon, it all fit perfectly.

After a speedy application of makeup, one final leg shave, and a generous spritz of black-currant body mist, Clawdeen stood on the lid of the toilet seat and consulted the mirror. A sixteen-year-old girl with an elegantly moody dress, tousled auburn curls, luminescent eyes, and the promise of Cleo's emerald earrings smiled back.

"Let's move!" she said, jumping down.

"I dunno," Lala said.

Clawdeen froze. *"What?"*

"I just don't think it's safe to go alone."

"Not safe or not *fun*?" Clawdeen dared.

Lala's eyes darkened. "What's that supposed to mean?" she snapped, unleashing the ire in *vampire*.

"It means you wanted to go when you thought Clawd was going," Clawdeen said, picking her clothes up off the floor and jamming them into her bag. Anything to keep her shaking hands busy.

"Because I thought he could protect us if something happened," Lala said, a little too loudly.

"Nothing's going to happen." Clawdeen turned on her phone and offered it to Lala. "Look." She read text after text from Cleo and Melody, urging them to hurry up and come to the party. "See? Everything is perfect."

Lala looked away from the screen, conflicted. "If Uncle Vlad heard I sneaked out, he'd kill me. And if my dad found out, he'd kill me again."

"How will they find out? Your uncle is in Portland, and your dad is on a yacht. Besides, you're already dead."

"It's not safe, Claw. Please don't do this. Maybe if we bring Clawd—?"

Clawdeen couldn't stand to whisper-argue any longer. She was already late for her own party. If she didn't leave soon, she'd miss it completely. "Forget it, La. I'll go alone."

She tossed her bags under the basin. Without another word, she slipped outside and raced for the back parking lot. In the distance, the maintenance truck, battered from years of hard labor, seemed up for anything. Including a fifteen-minute road trip with a semi-experienced, albeit determined, birthday girl.

Clawdeen unlocked the driver-side door, suddenly aware of how strange it felt to be one-on-one with the truck. Who was she kidding, thinking she could drive this thing by herself. Maybe Lala was right. Maybe she should ask Clawd. He could—*no!* Independence was not a dish served with two spoons. She would have to chew on this alone.

After a deep breath of oxygenated courage and another *where r u?* text from Cleo, Clawdeen opened the door. At least she knew the air bags worked.

"Going somewhere?"

The driver's seat was occupied.

Mom?

"Nice dress," Harriet said, gripping the wheel with both hands.

Ping!

Clawdeen ignored the text. "I can explain," she said, even though she couldn't. How would a woman who spent most of her life catering to six males understand the need for independence?

"I know about the party tonight," Harriet said, staring into the dark lot as if driving.

Clawdeen's heart *Titanic*-ed. "How?"

Harriet tugged her ears.

Ping!

Another text.

Is this really happening? Is my mother going to be the sole admirer of a dress that took months to make?

"Sorry," she muttered into the chilly breeze.

"Why, Deenie?"

Clawdeen considered her answer carefully. If only there was something she could say to gain her mother's sympathy. *I feel neglected.... This is me crying out for attention.... My life is in danger if I don't go through with this party....*

Harriet lifted her daughter's chin and looked her in the eye. "If you want to be treated like a grown-up, you have to act like a grown-up. So how about you get in the truck and tell me the truth."

Her mother had a point. Besides, she'd heard everything. There was nothing left to hide.

Clawdeen shuffled around to the passenger side and climbed in. Old coffee cups lay crushed by her party boots. A new pine-scented air freshener hung from the rearview mirror. The air between them was tense and frigid. But this was hardly the time to ask Harriet to crank the heat.

"Well?"

"The truth?" Clawdeen began. "The truth is I wanted a party. I wanted the friends, the dress, the presents, the dancing... everything. One night just for *me*. Not the triplets. Not Clawd. Not Leena. Not Rocks or Nino. Just me. And then, when everyone said it was too dangerous, I—" The corners of her mouth began to twitch. Clawdeen lowered her eyes, ashamed of her sixteen-year-old tears. "I'm just so over everyone telling me what's best for me." She wiped her cheeks. "It's like you all think I'm completely useless, but I'm not. I can work every power tool in Dad's shed. I can run faster than every boy in my grade. I get straight As, I can make my own clothes, and I've never once seen the inside of the principal's office or a police car—which is more than my brothers can say. I've never trashed a Denny's for running out of sausages, which is more than my sister can say. Oh, and my video blog has seven fans, and one of them said I'm a natural in front of the camera and a DIY maverick." The tears came faster now, wreaking havoc on her smoky lids. Not that it mattered. The parking lot was as far as she was going...probably for the next decade. "I guess I wanted to prove that I'm old enough to make my own decisions."

"Driving without a license is not a decision, Deenie. It's a crime."

"I was going to call a cab," she lied.

"And tell the driver what? To take you to a party that may or may not be a trap?" Harriet pulled the elastic from her ponytail and shook out her cinnamon-colored hair. It had grown at least an inch since dinner. "These are not *decisions*; they're mistakes."

"What's wrong with mistakes?" Clawdeen barked. She shifted to face the window and mumbled, "Not that I'd know. No one's ever let me make any."

After that the only sound between them was the *ping* of Clawdeen's text messages.

Harriet cleared her throat. "I understand how you feel."

Unsure that she'd heard correctly, Clawdeen turned back toward her mother. The cracked blue leather seat creaked in protest. "You do?"

Ping!

Harriet twisted the gold wedding band around her finger. "I used to be a lot like you when I was younger. I couldn't stand being bossed around by my mom and older sisters. So I worked as a waitress after school and saved up my money, and the summer before college, I backpacked through Europe. It was so liberating that I ended up staying. For the next two years I worked in restaurants, learned bits and pieces of different languages, and met the most incredible people."

Clawdeen was one part fascinated, two parts envious. It sounded like how flying must feel. Why hadn't her mom ever told her that before? "What made you come back?"

"A guy named Clawrk." Harriet grinned, suddenly looking girlish, the way she might have looked in those days. "We met at a café in Amsterdam and spent the next two weeks traveling together before he returned home to America. He begged me to return with him, but I refused. I told myself I wouldn't follow him, or any man. So he left and I stayed."

Clawdeen swiveled in her seat and faced her mother. "Just like that? Didn't he try to make you go with him?"

"Your father was too smart for that," Harriet snickered. "He told me I was making a big mistake, and then stepped aside and let me make it. Let's just say I was on a plane four days later." She paused and took Clawdeen's hand. "But your dad's a different guy now. He's not nearly as tough as he used to be. Do you know he cried during *Toy Story 3*?"

Clawdeen giggled.

Harriet sighed. "The hardest thing about being a parent is watching your kids make mistakes. Our instinct is to protect you. But you're right, Deenie. Sometimes we have to step aside and let you make them anyway. The best we can do is be there when you mess up."

Ping!

"Someone's trying to find you."

"It's probably Cleo and Melody wondering where I am." Clawdeen shut off her phone. They'd figure it out eventually.

"Buckle up."

"Huh?"

"Hurry," Harriet ordered, starting the engine. "We have a Sassy Sixteen to go to."

Clawdeen's heartbeat started to quicken. "What?"

"Maybe you're right," her mother said, turning on the heat. "Maybe everything will be fine. But I'll be right beside you, just in case it's not."

"Thanks, Mom," Clawdeen said, giving Harriet a giant hug. And then, "Can I drive?"

Harriet laughed. "Now you're pushing it," she replied, slowly backing out of the spot.

"Wait!" called a familiar voice. "Stop!"

Harriet stepped on the brake.

"If you're gonna do this, at least let me drive. You suck—" Lala appeared breathless at her window. "Oh, Mrs. Wolf. Sorry! I—I thought you were someone else." Her cheeks turned bright red. It was the most color she'd ever had.

Clawdeen leaned forward and waved. "It's okay, La. She's cool."

"You're not going to let that fabulous dress go to waste, are you?" asked Harriet.

Lala looked confused.

"Hop in," Harriet said. "We're late enough as it is."

Elated, the vamp did as she was told, squeezing up front beside Clawdeen.

"Woo-hoo!" they shouted as Harriet merged onto the highway and sped toward what might end up being the first—and most catastrophic—mistake of Clawdeen's life.

It was awesome.

CHAPTER TWENTY-ONE
PHAEDIN, FADE OUT

The train screeched into the Oregon City station.

"One more stop and we're there," Billy announced.

Frankie jammed her hands into the pockets of her black skinny jeans and turned away from the window. As pumped as she was for Portland, this was the only stop she had been thinking about. The goal—to get past it without sparking—involved not only her fingers but her memories too.

Billy's dark, almond-shaped eyes narrowed with concern. "You okay?"

"Voltage," she managed, wishing he would stop caring so much and just kiss her. Then she'd associate Oregon City with his lips instead of Brett's. She'd finally be able to move forward.

Sadly, VisiBilly wasn't a *make-the-first-move-on-a-train* kind of guy. Unlike InvisiBilly, the new Billy had gone to great lengths over the past week to prove he was a gentleman. And somewhere along the way, their friendship had become a courtship.

He wasn't able to "officially" start school until next semester. Still, Billy was at Merston every day at 3:35 PM with a black rose and an offer to walk Frankie home. He helped Viveka carry groceries in from the car. And always texted before he went to bed. They laughed less but talked more. After all, his practical jokes were mega-impractical now that he could be seen. Instead, striking looks and a clean-cut style became his calling card. And no one was more taken with Billy than her parents. They never would have let her see a Lady Gaga concert in Portland with Brett.

Ding. Ding.

The doors slid open. Frankie refused to think about the last time she had stepped through them. Refused to pay any attention to that Pop Rocks sensation erupting in her stomach. Refused to imagine how she'd feel if he got on the train right now. Refused to...

"Don't call my name, don't call my name, Alejandro..."

Four bleached-out blonds stepped onto the train belting the chorus of "Alejandro." Dressed in matching black shirtdresses and turquoise tights, with GAGA written in pink across their chests, they reminded Frankie why she was there. Suddenly, all thoughts of boys, kisses, and Pop Rocks tummies were left behind in Oregon City, where they belonged.

Still singing, the Gagas sat directly across the aisle from Billy. Tanned and dark-featured, wearing faded jeans, a white button-down with the sleeves rolled up, and gray-and-turquoise Nikes, he was unquestionably something to behold. But so were they. Loud, proud, and free of inhibitions, they were everything

Frankie aspired to be. And everything she could be...at least for tonight. Without further hesitation, she pulled her hands out of her pockets, knelt on her seat, and joined in.

"Don't wanna kiss, don't wanna touch..."

Nudging Billy, she urged him to sing along. And he did.

A briefcase-wielding man folded up his newspaper and switched cars. They took that as an invitation to sing louder. Soon, fans from all over the train began spilling in, each one a walking homage to Lady Gaga's unique sense of style. Billy, who didn't botch a single lyric, waved his arms as if conducting an orchestra. Every now and then he'd crack Frankie up with his falsetto and then go back to charming the other girls with his gleaming smile.

Carefree and uninhibited, Frankie had never felt so complete. She wasn't thinking about RADs or normies. Danger or safety. Hiding or protests. No one was. For the first time in her life, none of that mattered. Her only concern was having fun.

Arm in arm, the musical flash mob got through every song on *The Fame Monster* and half of *The Fame* before reaching their stop. While the train slowed, they crowded around the doors anxiously, primed and ready for the real thing.

"I never would have taken you for a monster," said one of the original blonds. "You look so...*mainstream*."

Billy burst out laughing. Frankie smiled at the irony.

Her outfit—black lace-up boots, black skinny jeans, a fitted black turtleneck, and a fur vest (inspired by Cleo's)—had been deliberate. Tonight she'd be the "normal" one. Perhaps then she'd understand what normies were so afraid of. But it was obvious by the way they'd accepted her that "mainstream versus monster" wasn't the issue. Connecting was.

Billy stepped onto the crowded platform. "You think the concert will be as fun as the train ride was?"

"I'm not sure it can be," Frankie said with a giggle.

"I'm glad you made me learn the words."

Frankie took his hand. "I'm glad about a lot of things."

The Rose Garden Arena generated more electricity than a Stein family reunion. The stadium was charged with joy, alive with energy circulated by thousands of bodies moving to the same beat. Frankie savored it like a gourmet meal.

Costume after costume, song after song, Lady Gaga kept everyone amped—so much so that Billy was sweating bronzer on the collar of his white shirt, a sobering reminder of how different they really were. Not that he seemed to care, or even notice. He put his arm around Frankie and sang along to "So Happy I Could Die" with the joy of someone who has just been released from prison.

During the chorus he drew Frankie closer. Casually, she licked her lips and allowed him to guide her. He turned to face her and smiled like a movie star. That tingly feeling right before two people make contact, when the brain shuts down and the body takes over, had begun. A Pop Rock or two burst inside her stomach. The crowd around them became dull and fuzzy....

And then she giggled.

Billy pulled back, his expression a mixture of confusion and pain.

"Sorry." Frankie giggled again. "It's nothing...."

"You sure?"

Frankie nodded with certainty. Billy closed his eyes and leaned toward her. She giggled again.

"*What?*"

"Sorry," she said, laughing. "It's just that up until last week, you were, like, my best friend, and now—"

He kissed her. Hard at first, as if proving a point, and then sweetly, as if proving his love. For someone with so little practice, he seemed to know what he was doing. Enough to distract her from the burned-caramel smell of his spray-tanned face.

Frankie mirrored his movements with accuracy and skill. Like a robotic fashionista who copied the trends without adding her own style, Frankie was uninspired. And yet she kept going, refusing to give up until she felt the fireworks. Because Billy was perfect for her. And she was—

Whooosh.

All of a sudden, Frankie's entire body began to sweat. Her flesh burned, her cheeks flushed. *Yes!* She leaned into him even more.

Billy pulled away. "What was *that*?" His shirt was stained orange. Dripping sweat, he wiped his forehead invisible. He dried the back of his hand on his jeans, leaving behind another orange stain—and a see-through spot on that hand.

"Uh-oh. Billy, your—"

"I know." He folded his arms across his chest. "I need to start investing in the good stuff," he said breezily.

Frankie snapped open her amp purse and handed him her makeup bag. "Here."

"How convenient," he mumbled, embarrassed. And he had every reason to be. Swapping spit in public was one thing, but makeup?

"Maybe you should go to the bathroom," she suggested.

Before he could answer, they were struck by a second blast of heat. Billy accidentally wiped away the other side of his forehead. Frankie, feeling all gooey, assumed she resembled a chunk of melted vanilla-mint fudge. The shock in Billy's semi-floating eyes confirmed her suspicion.

"What's going on?" Frankie asked, reaching for her neck seams.

Billy grabbed her hand before she could tug. "Let's get out of here."

She considered fighting for one more song, but she had promised her parents she wouldn't put herself in harm's way. Even at a Lady Gaga concert, cavorting in public with green skin and a semi-invisible friend had *harm's way* written all over it.

Like Cinderellas at midnight, they began racing for the privacy of their pumpkin. But their pumpkin was a public train.

Heads tucked, they hurried past girls who wore glasses covered in cigarettes, soda cans as curlers, bras made of caution tape, and see-through lace jumpsuits. They charged up the steps and ran out the exit. Suddenly everything was fluorescent bright. Leaving the pulsating venue for the stillness of the popcorn-scented corridors was jarring—like being unplugged mid-amp.

Everywhere, vendors peddling Gaga merchandise called to them, tempting them as they passed. Still, Frankie refused to look. The smell of popcorn had been replaced with burned caramel as the tanning solution dripped off Billy's body and onto hers. She considered lifting her gaze to assess the damage to his body, but she heard footsteps all around them. Some even sounded like they were coming toward them. Frankie and Billy ran faster and—

Oof!

Two male bodies collided into them. One of them was wearing mega-tread hiking boots, the laces singed by fire.

Frankie heard a boy's voice. "Whoa, dude, you guys look freaky."

Eyes lowered, she clenched her fists. She considered shocking him so they could escape.

But then the second boy spoke. *"Stein?"*

She sparked immediately.

"Brett?" She lifted her eyes, and sparks flew again.

"Come on, Frankie," Billy said, reaching for her. "We should go."

Frankie agreed. They needed to leave. *So why am I still standing here?*

"Dude, did my hiccups do that?" Heath asked, his red hair and lashes singed.

Billy looked down at his fading chest. He fastened the top button of his stained shirt with undetectable hands.

"Who's this guy?" Brett asked Frankie, more disturbed by what he could see than what he couldn't.

"Who do you *think* it is?" Billy said, answering for her.

"No way! Phaedin, is that you?" Brett's denim-blue eyes widened. "Frankie, is this who you moved on to?" He didn't sound arrogant, just sad.

"Yes," Billy blurted.

"No!" Frankie blurted, louder. "I mean, that's not what I mean. I—" She paused, wishing she were disappearing. *What do I mean?*

A security guard riding a Segway was zooming toward them.

"We need to get you guys out of here," Brett said. "Heath's sister is meeting us out front with the car."

He unzipped his navy sweatshirt, wrapped it around Frankie's shoulders, and lifted the hood to cover her face. "Billy, take off your shirt and—"

"What about his hair?" Heath pointed out.

"It's okay," Billy said, backing away. "A few seconds under the sink and it'll wash right out." His stained shirt fell to the floor. Next his pants, socks, and shoes, in a trail that led to the men's room.

The security guard rolled past, eyeing them suspiciously.

"You guys should go," Billy called, popping out his brown contact lenses.

"Billy, wait!" Frankie sniffed. *Don't be upset? Don't hate me? I never meant to hurt you? Can we still be friends? Will you ever forgive me? I wish I could change the way I feel? You deserve someone better? It hurts me more than it hurts you?* It all sounded so cliché. "You can't just stay here. Come with us. Please!"

"And miss the chance to sneak inside Lady Gaga's dressing room? Forget it."

Frankie giggled through her tears. *Why can't I make myself like him?*

"Go!" urged the floating brown hair. "If you leave now, you can probably make Clawdeen's party."

Brett tugged Frankie's arm.

"Are you going to be okay?" she tried one last time.

"Better than okay," Billy called, opening the bathroom door. "Did you see those hot backup dancers? Some of them might need help changing after the show."

"Killer." Heath chuckled.

Guilt gripped Frankie's heart space and squeezed. "Tonight was voltage," she said, meaning it.

"I know," Billy called. "Just no sparks."

As guilt got ready to squeeze again, Brett took Frankie's hand and pulled her away. She began melting all over again.

CHAPTER TWENTY-TWO
HAIR APPARENT

Harriet had to park in the Steins' cul-de-sac because her driveway was full. Not that Clawdeen minded. Showing up late to her own party was bad enough, but in a beat-up utility vehicle? *Fur-get about it.*

"Melody delivered like Domino's!" she gushed as they stepped onto Radcliffe Way. It was warmer here than at the inn. Or did it feel that way simply because she was about to be reunited with the people she loved?

"Our street looks like a used-car lot!" giggled Lala, black eyes wide with wonder.

"Just think," Harriet mused. "All these kids are here to celebrate you."

"See?" Clawdeen beamed. "I told you it would be okay."

Still, as Harriet pulled her daughter close, stubble poked through her black blouse and irritated Clawdeen's bare shoulders.

It was another reminder of the risk they were taking. Not only with the party but with the rounding moon. But why think about that when the electronic beat of "The Time" by the Black Eyed Peas was pulsating from the Wolfs' backyard?

"Woo-hoo!" howled Clawdeen. She and Lala raised their hands over their heads and began dancing and singing their way up the block.

"I had the time of my life, and I never felt this way before..."

Clawdeen couldn't have been happier. The closer they got, the more she wanted to run. But Cleo always said, "Guests of honor don't run; they appear." So Clawdeen and Lala decided to run and *appear* excited.

"Whoa," said Clawdeen, stopping. Dozens of luminary candle bags had been placed on her lawn, lighting a path to the tent in the backyard. Clawdeen recognized them immediately from the de Niles' New Year's Eve party, and she felt tremendous gratitude to Cleo (well, her *staff*) for all the hard work. The scene looked like one of those elegant celebrity affairs featured in *InStyle* magazine.

"It's beautiful," Harriet said, admiring her flickering front yard.

Suddenly, a tightening sensation gripped Clawdeen's scalp... held... and then released. Another growth spurt. Her auburn curls dropped, bounced, and then settled below her shoulders. Luckily, her mother had been too busy admiring the lights to notice. If she had, they'd be speeding back to the Hideout.

"Who's ready?" Clawdeen quickly asked.

Lala flashed a fang-tabulous smile, and they all linked arms.

Rounding the side of her house in a DIY dress and sparkling booties, guided by the luminaries and the sound of Bruno Mars's latest single, Clawdeen was having a major Dorothy moment. That Kansas normie had gotten one thing right: There's no place like home.

CHAPTER TWENTY-THREE
PAIN IN THE SASS

The golden tent cast a royal glow on the forty-plus guests as DJ Duhman spun things sweaty.

His gear consisted of an iPod touch, a thin black wire, a headset microphone, and refrigerator-sized speakers. His "booth"— a bronze-plated, hieroglyphic-covered tomb with black-lacquered lion's paws for legs—had been relegated to the far corner of the tent because Cleo swore he smelled like bananas. And apparently Clawdeen couldn't stand bananas.

I hope she likes Egyptian-themed parties and Middle Eastern munchies....

"We have another contest coming up in T-minus five minutes," announced Duhman. Rainbow-colored dreadlocks hung slack around his pasty face like deflated balloons as he scrolled through his playlist, fading out "The Time" and turning up Bruno Mars.

Melody sat alone in a gold-wrapped chair at a gold-wrapped

table observing the scene. Dancing was the second-to-last thing she felt like doing tonight. Losing Jackson was the last. At least everyone else was having fun. Julia Phelps was cutting a reed with Haylee and the rest of Bekka's ex-friends. Three RAD guys she recognized from the meetings at Frankie's house had formed a conga line with a trio of normie girls from the Lactose-Free Zone. And bangle-clanging arms waved through the air as bodies dressed in colorful dry-clean-only fabrics collided peacefully. Granted, most of the RADs were no-shows, and those who were there wore disguises. But, still, for a town full of supposed "closed-minded normies," everyone seemed to blend like polyester and cotton.

Cleo finger-pulled Mason Unger off the dance floor. The leggy basketball player plodded behind her dutifully, like a Great Dane being walked by a child. Ten minutes with the exotic beauty and he was already wrapped—just like the jewel garland around her bangs, the gold silk around her legs, and the ruby-red strapless mini around her curves.

Melody raced past the mounted photo exhibit of Clawdeen through the ages, managing to stop the couple before they slithered out of the tent. "Any word?" she asked, shouting over the blaring music.

Cleo's royal blue heels screeched to a stop by the gift table. "If I had *word*, do you think I'd be with—" She tilted her head toward Mason.

"Not from *Deuce*," Melody snipped. "From Clawdeen. I hope she's okay. She hasn't answered any of my texts."

Cleo smirked. "Don't get your feathers in a ruffle," she said,

213

taking an obvious jab at Melody's feather-covered dress and matching hair adornments. "Deenie's not going to let anything keep her away from this party."

"Well, she's over an hour late, and I think some of the guys are starting to leave."

"*Ka*," Cleo said, dismissing them with a wave of her bejeweled hand. "That's what guys do. They leave. Get used to it. I did." She tugged her Great Dane, and off they walked.

I can't get used to it! I have to keep trying. Unlike you, I'm not going to give up. No matter how many times I fail. At least not until tomorrow, Melody wanted to scream. But her emotional breakdown would have to wait. Finding Jackson was still the priority, even though it seemed like he didn't want to be found.

The plan was to deliver her message of acceptance during a birthday toast to Clawdeen. After a few words about the guest of honor, Melody would persuade everyone to live in harmony and to fight to keep Ms. J at Merston.

Cleo had told her that Mr. D's planes had to wait until the airport was closed before taking off, so they could fly under the radar. According to Melody's research, the last *legal* flight wasn't scheduled to depart for three more hours. There was still time to manipulate the crowd, get them to charge McNary and stop the plane. If Clawdeen ever showed…

Melody gripped her roiling stomach. This edge-of-her-seat lifestyle wasn't agreeing with her digestion. Nor was the onion-raisin-cinnamon smell wafting from Beb and Hasina's serving trays.

"All right, party people, who's ready for another contest?" asked DJ Duhman.

"Woo-hoo!" answered the flush-faced crowd. All the guests except a six-pack of boys who were hiding out by the photo exhibit assured the DJ they were up for it.

"Ha! I love it! O-kayyy. Ladies, go out there and find a guy who turns! Your! Head!"

"Whip My Hair" began thumping from the speakers. Girls started pulling elastics and bobby pins from their updos. By the time the lyrics kicked in, they were speed-swinging their locks Willow Smith–style. A bit more force and the tent would have blown over.

Melody couldn't help wondering what she'd be doing if Jackson were there. Since neither was really one for whipping of any kind, they probably would have been laughing on the sidelines as dizzy contestants lost their balance and bashed into one another. Either that or—

"Wolf! Wolf! Wolf!" chanted the six-pack.

Clawdeen! She made it!

The sooner Melody greeted the woman of the hour, the sooner she could make her toast and stop Ms. J's plane from taking off. Her motives were slightly self-serving, but only in the short term. Long term, her push to unite Salem would benefit them all.

Melody waved Cleo in from the elm just outside the tent. "She's here!"

The mummy flashed a wait-a-second finger. She was on the phone, pacing back and forth while Mason leaned against the gold-wrapped trunk, picking his nails.

"Wolf! Wolf! Wolf!"

Despite Clawdeen's arrival, the dance floor was still packed. Melody waved again to Cleo, who responded by pointing at her phone and then flashing a thumbs-up. Deuce had finally called— and Cleo's smile was so bright that it shined a floodlight on the fact that Jackson had not.

"Don't let haters keep me off my grind, keep my head up and I know I'll be fine…"

The song was almost over. All Melody had to do was greet Clawdeen and get everyone's attention before the DJ played another one. Then she could give her speech and still have plenty of time to get everyone down to McNary to stop Ms. J's plane.

With renewed urgency, she hurried for the chanting six-pack of normies. She quickly realized they were part of the fraud-squad that had sabotaged her petition with fake names. But Melody held her tongue. She'd lecture them soon enough.

"'Scuse me," she insisted, forcing her way into their tight huddle. But the auburn-haired beauty was nowhere to be found. Not the real one, at least. The photographic version, however, was everywhere, mounted on a gigantic canvas. Clawdeen as a bald newborn, a thumb-sucking baby, a big-eared toddler, dressed up as a superhero, a tap dancer, a tool-belt-wearing tween. Each picture was more adorable than the next. At least, the photos had been adorable before the boys arrived.

But the pen that was once tied to the guestbook had been used to draw long fingernails on Clawdeen's hands. Pointy teeth jutted from her mouth, and scribbles of hair covered her face.

216

Melody swallowed hard to avoid barfing up her baba gha-noush. How could she have let this happen?

"Wolf! Wolf! Wolf!" shouted the boys. They had moved on to the photo of Clawdeen at her middle school graduation. A guy in a pit-stained polo had drawn a full moon over her head and was now adding a squirrel hanging from her mouth.

Cleo finally came running over, a pair of emerald earrings clenched in her fist. "Where is she?" she shouted, phone still to her ear. And then she saw the photos. "Oh. My. Geb," she muttered, disconnecting the call.

Melody looked away in shame. She knew exactly how these normies felt about RADs. Their fake petition signatures had made that perfectly clear. Still, she'd persuaded them to come. Not to please Clawdeen but to please herself. Not to save Ms. J but to save her relationship with Jackson.

Melody couldn't stand by and watch any longer. She ordered the guys to stop. But they couldn't hear her above the voice of the DJ, who was urging the contestants to "make like the dog and whippet!"

"Freeze!" she tried again. But the guys kept drawing. The only ones who froze were the three people standing behind them.

Mrs. Wolf, Lala, and Clawdeen.

CHAPTER TWENTY-FOUR
BIG PACK ATTACK

"My pictures!" Harriet shouted, her orange-brown eyes searching for someone to blame.

Clawdeen didn't have to see the ink smudges on Colton Tate's fingertips to know that he was responsible. He, along with Darren, Tucker, Rory, Nick, and Trevor, had been tormenting her ever since she joined their precious Merston High track team. She'd never put them on the invite list. Why were they even there? They blew spitballs in her hair, "accidentally" bumped into her, and even taped crude sketches of male anatomy to her locker. Cleo insisted they had a six-way crush on her, but Clawdeen knew better. As Coach Paige liked to say, she ran faster than a toddler's nose. And that left the boys feeling more disposable than tissue. But why couldn't they have let it go? Just for one night? Instead, they turned away and faced the crowded dance floor, feigning innocence with wide eyes, casual whistles, and hands jammed into the front pockets of their jeans.

"Oh my Geb, I know exactly how you feel," Cleo said, pulling Clawdeen into an amber-scented hug. "You've been waiting and waiting for this party, and even though it's super raging and the decorations are golden, something like *this*"—she gestured to the photo display—"had to happen and ruin your big moment."

Clawdeen hugged Cleo harder. *Yes, that's exactly how I feel.*

"It's like me and Deuce. I've been waiting and waiting for him to call me, and when he finally did, I saw your messed-up pictures and accidentally hung up on him. So my big moment was ruined too."

Clawdeen pulled away and glared into her friend's topaz-colored eyes. *Deuce? You're making this about Deuce?* her raised eyebrows asked.

Catching on, Cleo bit her bottom lip apologetically and opened her palm. "Earrings?"

Two spectacular pear-shaped hunks of emerald, wrapped in gold wire, winked their good-time intentions. But Clawdeen looked away. The jewels were far too fabulous for her mood.

Beneath her beautiful DIY wrap dress, with its iridescent sheen and black metallic slash, a kaleidoscope of emotions revolved and collided. Rage smashed into frustration; frustration struck devastation; devastation hit regret; then regret teamed up with shame and sucker punched Clawdeen in the heart. All she could do was stare at her defiled baby photos and fight the urge to cry.

Lala was gripping her now, trying to shake out a reaction the way she might dislodge a soda can that was stuck in a vending machine. "Deenie, say something."

But Clawdeen couldn't speak. Words would bring tears. And nothing says *you win* like a mascara-smudged face and a salt-stained DVF knockoff.

Harriet began pulling the photos off the canvas. Her fingernails had grown since they left the inn, making it harder for her to grip the gold tacks. But she kept at it, clearly needing something to claw at.

The DJ declared Haylee the winner of the hair-whipping contest and then began playing the *Glee* cast version of "I'll Stand By You" (even though Clawdeen had e-mailed him weeks ago to say no slow songs before ten o'clock). Everyone cleared the dance floor. One by one, friends came up to her offering sweaty, deodorant-scented hugs, birthday wishes, and outfit compliments.

Clawdeen accepted them graciously but found it hard to move her mouth to smile. Her heart was too heavy. It weighed everything down.

"Hey, where did everyone go?" asked DJ Duhman. "Come on, *I want you back*!"

The ancient Jackson Five song came through the speakers with a burst, and everyone rushed onto the dance floor with a delighted scream.

"I'm so sorry," said Melody Carver, gray eyes wide with horror. "This is all my fault."

Her dress was covered in the most vibrant and luxurious feathers Clawdeen had ever seen. Yet their placement was way off—too many around the neck and not enough hanging from the hem—but it was nothing a DIY expert and her Singer couldn't fix.

"Omigod, did *they* put those on you?" Lala asked, concerned. "That is beyond not okay."

"No, they're mine," Melody said, and then kept babbling about some petition and Jackson and how she thought she could make things better for them. "My plan was to get everyone together and then use my power to persuade them to accept—"

"Power?" Lala asked. "What *power*?"

"My voice," Melody whispered, pointing at her long neck. "I can make people *do things*...."

"It's true, don't let the shoes fool you," Cleo said, pointing to Melody's black high-top Converse. "This girl has got it going on."

Pressure began to build behind Clawdeen's fingertips.

"Melody, go," Cleo said, nudging the normie toward the group of track boys. "Make them apologize to Clawdeen."

"Yeah, right." Clawdeen rolled her eyes, knowing how dedicated they were to humiliating her.

Lala bit her thumbnail.

"Go," Cleo urged.

Melody seemed to consider it for a moment. Then she rolled back her shoulders and marched toward them, semi-tied shoelaces dragging alongside her. She tapped Rory on the back. He turned around to face her. She whispered something in her ear and then did the same to Tucker, Nick, Trevor, and Darren. One by one, they approached Clawdeen and apologized for ruining her pictures. They apologized for the spitballs, the dirty drawings, the cafeteria collisions, and their overall bad behavior.

Clawdeen stood before them dumbfounded. Melody definitely had a power.

"Hey, when did *you* get here?" asked Colton, his beady eyes glinting mischief. He'd come from the dance floor.

Clawdeen's heart began to pump Red Bull instead of blood. The skin on the back of her neck tightened. He was the worst one of all.

"Hey, guys," he panted, wiping his sweaty forehead on the sleeve of his button-down. "The guest of honor has arrived!" And then, "Let's have a round of *a-claws* for—"

"Omigod, dude," shouted Nick. "Look at her neck!"

"She's like a Chia Pet!"

"She needs a Chia vet!"

Clawdeen's scalp cramped and then released. Auburn curls bounced and settled on her collarbone.

The guys began reaching for their cell phones.

"CNN is gonna be all over this!"

"So is Animal Planet!"

"Um, Mrs. Wolf," Cleo called, slightly panicked. No one except Clawdeen's family had ever witnessed her transition. Not even her best friends.

Harriet turned away from the photos and gasped. But all Clawdeen could do was glare at the boys and growl. One swipe with her nails and she could scar them for life. One shove and they'd be lying on their backs in the middle of the dance floor. One roar and they'd be crying for their mommies, begging for a diaper change. Imagining it all brought levity back into Clawdeen's heart. She grinned. It would be the last time they'd ever bother her, that was for sure.

Lala grabbed Clawdeen by the arm. "Let's get you out of here."

"No, wait!" Clawdeen said, standing her ground. She was done with hiding. The Wolfs had spent generations avoiding public transitions—it was their greatest fear. But why? They could outrun, outfight, and out-eavesdrop any normie who stood in their way. Their metabolisms alone could bring Hollywood to its knees. Weren't they the ones with all the power? Shouldn't normies fear *them*?

"Let's go!" Harriet insisted, lifting her daughter by the waist and rushing her outside the tent. Lala and Cleo followed.

"Put me down!" Clawdeen flailed, remembering how Clawd had carried her from Cleo's house days earlier in the same humiliating way. "I *said* PUT! ME! DOWN!"

She managed to wriggle free by the gold-wrapped elm tree.

"Look!" Harriet held out a compact mirror.

Lala and Cleo stood beside her, hemorrhaging nervous energy. But Clawdeen was strangely calm as she stared at her reflection for the second time that night. Only now her neck was wrapped in luxurious auburn fur. Her curls were touching the top of her dress's built-in bra. And her nails were Rihanna-long. *What's not to love?*

"Come on, Deenie, you've made your big mistake. Can we go now?" Harriet urged, her eyes turning more orange than brown. She too would start transitioning soon.

"Why, Mom? Everyone knows. What's the point—?"

"Hey!" called a chipper voice from the luminary path. Frankie Stein was speed-walking toward them, her arms already open for a hug. Brett and Heath were a few steps behind her. "Happy birthday! I'm so sorry we're late. We were at the Lady Gaga concert, and then I had to stop off and touch up my makeup, and—" Her fingers sparked. She stopped walking, and her hug-arms fell to her sides. "Your fur!"

"I know." Clawdeen giggled. "It kind of just happened."

"These earrings would really pop now," Cleo said, opening her palm.

This time Clawdeen took them.

Harriet folded her arms across her chest and sighed. It sounded like a soft growl.

"Happy birthday," said Brett shyly.

"Yeah." Heath waved. "Happy birthday."

Clawdeen, Lala, and Cleo exchanged a glance.

Frankie took Brett's hand. "It's okay. He's one of the good guys."

Lala smiled with relief, her ultrawhite fangs gleaming in the moonlight.

All of a sudden, a series of familiar piercing beats filled the yard. Something that felt like a rocket shot straight up from her toes to her brain. The DJ was playing their song.

"Ahhhh!" screamed Lala.

"Ahhhh!" answered Clawdeen.

"*If you're one of us then roll with us*," they rapped along with Ke$ha.

Cleo's cell phone rang. It was Deuce. She quickly answered, shouted "I'll call you back," and then hung up. Then she sang, "*We runnin' this town…*"

Frankie joined in. "*You don't wanna mess with us…*"

And before they knew what was happening, Clawdeen had

grabbed her friends and run with them across her lawn to the dance floor. She was finally going to be like her European cousins and let it all hang out.

Forcing her way through a giant mass of gyrating bodies, Clawdeen landed right in the middle, just in time for the chorus.

They sang as loud as they could, their voices blending with the dozens of others around them. The track guys were documenting the scene with their cell phone cameras, and instead of hiding, the girls gave them exactly what they wanted. Lala smiled wide for their tiny lenses, Clawdeen twirled her fur, and Frankie wiped her makeup off on their uptight button-downs. Soon Brett was dancing beside her, helping to clear away the last bits of Silly Putty–colored goop from behind her ears. Haylee worked her way into their circle and wiggled up against Heath. A shot of fire rushed from his mouth, and everyone cheered. Harriet was among them. Frankie lifted her fingers above the crowd and sparked to the beat. The track boys made a circle around Clawdeen as she danced. They danced too.

Songs melted into one another, and the party showed no signs of slowing down. The Wolf brothers arrived, thanks to a call from Harriet and strict orders to let their hair down. When all was said and done, DJ Duhman had logged three hours of overtime.

Clawdeen promised her mother she'd clean out her life savings to cover the extra cost, and Harriet acquiesced. After all, six hundred dollars was a small price to pay for freedom.

Life was normal again. Only everything had changed.

Billy couldn't imagine anything more depressing than riding back to Salem alone, invisible as usual. Every screech and hiss of the train would torture him, a cruel reminder that he hadn't noticed those sounds earlier. How could he have? He'd been having too much fun.

He'd considered asking Candace to pick him up, but Frankie had his phone. At least that's what he told himself. In truth, he was too ashamed. How could he possibly explain surrender to a girl who had never lost?

So after a speedy hair rinse, Billy ran like mad to sneak a ride home with Heath's sister.

Jammed in the backseat of Harmony's Prius, pressed up against the cold window, he felt like an insect Mr. Stein might mash between glass slides and study under a microscope. Only worse. At least the insect would be dead and wouldn't have to listen to Frankie giggle-kiss another guy.

He wanted to hate her. Wished he could hate her. But by the time they got to Radcliffe Way, he loved her even more. And wanted to kill Brett a little less.

He could tell that Frankie and Brett really cared about each other. They always had. Their time apart had been a casualty of war. Frankie's interest in Billy was just a panacea for her pain, sparked by her mother's advice to stick to her own kind. It was hard to hear but good to know.

Billy also learned that Frankie considered him her best friend. And she insisted that Brett be okay with that relationship. Brett promised he was. He said he had always liked Billy, even though he knew the feelings weren't exactly mutual.

They are now.

Harmony had dropped them off at Clawdeen's, where for the last hour Frankie and Brett had been dancing and swapping sparks—sparks Billy and Frankie never had.

He watched from the sidelines as his friends finally took a stand. United as a community, they were letting their freak flags fly. It was the end of an era and the beginning of a new one. Anything was possible, simply because no one could prove it wasn't.

Awash with hope, Billy couldn't help wondering what it would be like to kiss a girl who wanted to kiss him back. Would she be a normie or a RAD? Would she favor a spray tan or prefer his natural state? Would—

227

Suddenly, "Invisible" by Ashlee Simpson began to play.

He laughed. Candace had been mocking him with that song since the day they met. Leaving it on his voice mail, blasting it in her car, singing it when they walked down the street together and marveling at strangers' reactions. He smiled, no longer ashamed.

"What's so funny?" Someone giggled.

"Who is that?" he asked, looking around. Billy touched his hair. *Did I miss a spot?*

Something hissed. Like a leaking tire or a can of hair spray. Seconds later a girl appeared beside him. Or rather, her face. She had pale ice-blue eyes and full lips. A tendril of violet hair butterfly-kissed her cheek.

"I'm Spectra," she said with a smile, then vanished. With another hiss, her hand appeared, extended. After they shook, it disappeared.

"Can you *see* me?" Billy asked, and then, realizing, quickly covered his—

"No!" She giggled again. "Don't worry, I can only see a blob of heat. Unless I spray you. Then I can—"

"No!" Billy stepped away from the voice. "No spray... at least nothing below the neck."

"Deal," she said, unleashing a sugar cookie–scented mist over his face.

"What is that stuff?"

"Smells good, right?" she said, spraying her face again so he could see her smile. "So far I have thirty-three different scents. I—" She blushed and then faded. "Wow. You're..."

"What?"

"...not ugly."

"Why? You thought I would be?"

"I didn't know what to think."

"You've been thinking about me?" he asked, grateful she couldn't see his gigantic grin.

"Only since that practical joke you pulled."

"When I dressed up like Frankie and went to see Brett in the hospital?"

"No. When you tied Mr. Barnett's shoelaces together."

Billy would have sparked if he could. "You mean in *eighth* grade?"

"Yes."

"You wanna dance?" he asked.

"I was hoping you'd finally ask," she said. It sounded like she was smiling.

The beginning of a new era indeed.

CHAPTER TWENTY-FIVE
THE SHOCK EXCHANGE

Frankie and Brett waved good-bye as another carload of guests drove up Radcliffe Way. The night air felt different against her makeup-free cheeks—like washing dishes with bare hands instead of wearing rubber gloves.

"I still can't believe they can see your real face," Brett said, waving. He put his arm around her shoulders and began strolling down the block toward the cul-de-sac. "This had to have been the best night of your life."

"Why?" Frankie asked, swinging her amp bag. "Because we're back together?"

He chuckled. "Yup."

But Frankie knew Brett was referring to an evening that had started with a Lady Gaga concert and ended in an unprecedented dance party—one that had allowed the RADs to let loose in front of normies. It was all she'd ever wanted. And yet for some reason Frankie felt restless and unsatisfied. As if her good fortune was undeserved. Like a slacker teen who'd inherited a trust fund or a celebrity who'd found fame by starring on a reality show.

Brett stopped walking. "What's wrong?" he asked, searching her exposed face.

"I can't believe Billy missed it," she said. She wished he could have been there. "I hope he's okay." What she really wanted to say was she hoped she hadn't broken his heart. But it was obvious by the way Brett looked at her that he understood.

"I know what it feels like to miss Frankie Stein." He sighed, taking her hand. "And it's not easy."

"Is that supposed to make me feel better?" she asked, pulling away.

"No, I guess not." Brett chuckled. "What I mean is, you're a good friend and he's lucky to have you. He knows that. Anyway, no guy wants to be with a girl if she's not into him. So you did him a favor. Really."

Frankie appreciated Brett's trying to make her feel better, but the only thing that would relieve the ache in her heart space was the knowledge that her friend was okay. Besides, Billy-guilt was only half the problem.

"Do you think I'm a failure?" she asked, wishing she was strong enough to hide her insecurities. But something about Brett made her feel safe. Maybe it was the color of his blue eyes; like denim, they held the promise of time.

"A *failure*?"

Frankie recalled the conversation she had overheard between her parents on the day she was born:

"She's so beautiful and full of potential, and it..." Her mother sniffed. "It just breaks my heart that she'll have to live...you know...like us."

"What's wrong with us?" her father asked. Yet something in his voice suggested that he already knew.

Viveka snickered. "You're kidding, right?"

"Viv, things won't be like this forever," Viktor said. "Times will change. You'll see."

"How? Who's going to change them?"

"I don't know. Someone will...eventually."

"Well, I hope we're around to see it," she said, sighing.

"I was supposed to be that person," Frankie said, clenching her jaw to keep from crying. "I was supposed to change things for her. But every time I tried, I messed up."

Brett lifted her chin so their eyes met. "Tonight RADs and normies were together. Just like your mother wanted."

"Yeah, but I had nothing to do with it. It was all Clawdeen. I was too busy thinking about boys and concerts and fun and—"

"Isn't that what you're supposed to be thinking about?"

Frankie considered the TV shows, movies, and books for girls her age. And he was right. Boys, music, and fun were a big part of them all. Changing the world single-handedly? Not so much.

"Besides, don't you think everything you've done helped make this possible? You were the spark that started it, Frankie." He brushed a loose piece of hair off her face. "Tonight, while we were dancing, were you happy?" he asked, moonlight reflecting off his spiky black hair.

Could he be any more mint?

Frankie thought about wiping off her makeup to the beat of Ke$ha, ripping the sleeves of her shirt to Pink, snapping and zapping whitish-blue bolts from her fingertips, making out with her normie boyfriend, and melting a little more every time his hands skimmed her bolts. "It was the most voltage time I've ever had," she said.

"Then you *did* give your mother what she wanted," he said.

Frankie hopped up on her toes and kissed him. Her green face was pressed against his white one. Right in the middle of Radcliffe Way as car after car drove by.

And the best part? Nobody seemed the least bit interested.

CHAPTER TWENTY-SIX
JACKS-ON!

It happened just the way it did in cartoons. Only instead of a silly wabbit following the buttery-rich smell of warm chicken, Melody caught wind of a tune.

It began softly, a lyrical yawn. And expanded into haunting, drawn-out notes that lasted as long as an exhale and then trailed off like smoke. They sounded effortless, like breathing. Yet inspired, like poetry. *Can anyone else at the party hear this?* It seemed unlikely, with the music blaring. So why could she?

Clawdeen had been whisked away by her mother. Melody had started following them toward the elm tree....

But the music—it was entering her now. Seeping into her pores, like sweating in reverse. Swelling and fading...swelling and fading...keeping perfect time with the rise and fall of Melody's abdomen. Her heart had become its metronome; its voice, her master. And this master wanted her out of there.

Gentle but sure, the tune drew her along like a lazy river's current. Melody followed its call down Radcliffe Way. Her thoughts no longer ricocheted between Jackson and Clawdeen. The music was all she heard. All she wanted to hear. Her mind was empty, peaceful. She could have followed the sound for days.

But it stopped immediately after she knocked on the door to the white cottage. The lazy river turned back into a stormy sea, sloshing her thoughts around like ill-fated sailors.

What am I doing here?

The woman with the seafoam-green eyes was the last person Melody wanted to see. An *I-told-you-so* lecture was useless at this point. She was all too aware of destiny's fragility. She had watched it come crashing down all over Clawdeen. Jackson's leaving would be Melody's cosmic punishment. And she would accept it with grace.

As she turned to leave, the door opened. Surprisingly, the eyes that greeted her were hazel.

"Melody?"

"Ms. J?" she said. And then, "Omigod, Ms. J!" Not caring whether she was crossing a boundary or not, she pulled the woman in for a hug. "What are you doing here? Is this real? Are you real?" she asked, not letting go.

"Yes, it's real." Ms. J laughed.

"But how—?"

"We were about to take off when I got a message from Mr. D. It seems as though everyone is ready to take a stand." She smiled, her red matte lipstick perfectly intact, as always. "And you know what they say about safety in numbers."

Why didn't Jackson tell me? Why didn't he . . .

"Jackson's in the shower," Ms. J said. "You can come in and wait if you want. I know he'll be happy to see you."

"That's okay," Melody said, tired of feeling pathetic. If Jackson wanted to talk to her, he would have called. And he hadn't. "Things are kind of crazy at Clawdeen's, so—"

"It's not his fault, Melody."

"Huh?" she asked, with a firefly's flash of hope.

"It's mine." The teacher sighed. "I blasted him with heat for two weeks straight."

"What?"

"Jackson would have found a way to contact you, and it was crucial no one knew where we were hiding," Ms. J said. "Not even you."

"So you turned him into D.J.?"

"Yup. It was nice, actually. We bonded. And Jackson doesn't remember a thing. But the poor guy was *sweaty.*"

Melody laughed. Jackson was upstairs taking a shower!

What if she hadn't invited those normies to Clawdeen's Sassy? Would he still be upstairs taking a shower? Would Clawdeen have eventually found another excuse to go public? If she had, would her brothers have joined her? Would Lala and Cleo? Would it have ended the same way—with the support of the entire community? Would it have brought Jackson home?

It was impossible to know. But it certainly made a great case for messing with destiny.

"What happened to the woman who was living here?" Melody asked.

236

"You really took a shine to each other, didn't you?"

"Not really, no."

"Oh," Ms. J said, turning away from the door. She quickly returned with a sealed envelope. "Well, she left this for you."

"Really?"

"Come in and sit. I've got some unpacking to do. Jackson will be right down."

Melody followed Ms. J inside the chilly home and settled into the dusty velvet couch in the living room. It hugged her like a long-lost friend.

Once alone, she opened the letter. A feather—olive and blue, with a golden tip—fell out and landed in her lap.

Dearest Melody,

A good mother knows what's best for her child. But a great mother does what's best, even when it's not good for her. And that, my daughter, is why I gave you up. A day hasn't passed when I don't feel the searing pain of my decision. Yet I have no regrets. I wanted you to be free to make your own choices. To live your own life. And to mess it up from time to time. But you wouldn't have had that freedom if I raised you. Because I too have a powerful voice. It's much more persuasive than yours.

We are Sirens. Bird-women. Our songs are seductive, and our words are powerful. Yours will grow stronger as you get older, so use your voice wisely. Destiny is not ours to control. Remember, real power comes not from the Siren's song but from her heart.

Until next time.

All my love,
Marina

P.S. What happened to your beautiful nose? Did you break it? If so, how? FYI, I broke mine playing football right after you were born. Note: Girls like us should never yell "Pass!" unless we mean it. Anyway, Dr. Carver fixed me right up. During a follow-up appointment, he mentioned how hard he and his wife had been try-ing to adopt. I knew they would love you as much as I do.

Relieved, Melody buried her face in her hands and began to laugh. It was the last reaction she thought she'd have to a note like this. But the weight of a hundred questions had been lifted, leaving her giddy and light. It all made sense: her voice, the feathers, Marina, her parents, her place in the world. Her place in the community. Her place in Jackson's heart. She had her answers. And each one proved the same thing: that she was loved.

Upstairs the pipes squeaked, and the shower stopped running. Jackson was drying off. He wouldn't smell like pastels when he hugged her; he would smell like soap. They wouldn't talk about where he'd been but rather where they were going. And they wouldn't need to find Melody's place among the RADs; they would know. She was a Siren. She belonged with them.

Melody thought back to the day she had arrived in Salem. She'd gazed out the window of her father's BMW, thinking that the minute she stepped out of the car she'd be starting a new life. Now, with the sound of Jackson's footsteps creaking overhead and Marina's letter clutched in her hand, she realized she had been wrong. Her new life hadn't started then.

It was starting now.

DON'T MISS THE NEXT BOOK

MONSTER HIGH 4

BACK AND DEADER THAN EVER

COMING SPRING 2012!

Enroll in
Monster High

OCTOBER 2011